# THE VOICE OF
# OLDER ADULTS

The Voice of Older Adults

Published by Life Rattle Press, Toronto, Canada

"Sunday Dinner," by Virginia Ashberry, was
previously published in *Time and Place*, Volume 4, Issue 2.

Library and Archives Canada Cataloguing in Publication

The voice of older adults / collected by Virginia Ashberry and Jeff Griffiths.

(New writers series, ISSN 1200-5266)
ISBN 978-1-987936-75-9 (softcover)

1. Older people's writings, Canadian (English)--Ontario--Hamilton.
2. Short stories, Canadian (English)--Ontario--Hamilton. 3. Canadian fiction
(English)--Ontario--Hamilton. 4. Canadian fiction (English)--21st century.
I. Ashberry, Virginia, 1952-, editor II. Griffiths, Jeff, 1957-, editor
III. Series: Life Rattle new writers series

PS8235.S45V65 2018   C813'.010892850971352090512   C2018-905599-5

# THE VOICE OF OLDER ADULTS

Collected by
Virginia Ashberry
and Jeff Griffiths

LIFE RATTLE PRESS  TORONTO, CANADA

# Table of Contents

# JEFF GRIFFITHS

*Jeff Griffiths teaches creative writing courses at Mohawk College in Hamilton. His short fiction and poetry has been published in various literary journals. He won the Arts Hamilton award for short fiction in 2007 and 2008. He was short listed for* Fiddlehead*'s short fiction award in 2017. He edits fiction for the Hamilton-based arts journal* Time and Place. *He has written and presented many short memoir stories for a bi-monthly charity event.*

## FOREWORD

In the summer of 2015, I was asked by James Gillett (Associate Dean, Grad Studies and Research, Faculty of Social Sciences) to facilitate a memoir group for older adults, at McMaster University. It was a program for the study of aging.

I sat with a group of eight on a Saturday for four hours and again with a new group the following week. We discussed memoirs, life, writing, and I gave one writing prompt. "Write about a pivotal time in your life," I said. "You have thirty minutes." This brought many good words to the surface.

Over the summer they were to write about an important time in their lives where "resilience" was a factor.

We met again at the end of August to hear what everyone had written. The results were amazing.

James and I met with Laura Lukasik at the Hamilton Public Library to discuss the idea of writing sessions for older adults. Laura said, "Let's do it." She looked at me and said, "Would you like to run the sessions?" Of course I did, and have loved every minute of it.

I've never had a more emotional and rewarding learning experience before working with this gang of creative people.

This collection of writing from the Central Library Group is a true reflection of creative minds putting pen to paper.

# VIRGINIA ASHBERRY

*Virginia Ashberry has been living and writing in Hamilton for the past six years. What a cool place to do this, eh?*

## SUNDAY DINNER

In the 1950s, we always had roast beef for dinner on Sundays. A roast every week proved to my father's satisfaction that he could keep his wife, two sons and one daughter well; proved to him that the poverty of his childhood would never be revisited.

Ours was not a good roast. Not that I knew a good cut of beef yet. I was thirty years old before a friend introduced me to rump roast, eye of round, and prime rib. No, every Sunday we had a cheap cut, short rib or chuck, virtually stewed in a big black enamel roasting pan, lid on, two cups of water and a big blob of catsup poured over the meat. Cooked more by steaming than roasting, a process that leached every scent of flavor from the meat after four hours at 375 degrees Fahrenheit.

And on most Sundays, an hour before dinner, about the same time that Tinkerbell glazed our black and white television screen with *The Wonderful World of Disney*, Mom would dump five pounds of peeled and quartered potatoes, four onions peeled and quartered and two pounds of carrots into the simmering dark brown slush around the roast, slopping the chunks about in the juice till they all glistened. Then she'd put the big black lid back on and shove the pan back into the oven.

"There's never much gravy if you cook the vegetables in with the roast, they take all the browning out of the drippings," she'd recite, even if no one was in the kitchen to hear. Still standing there, hands on her hips, the long, dirty white tea towel used instead of oven mitts dangling from her right hand, she'd state: "I'll have to use Bisto if we're going to have any gravy at all," then sighing in defeat, "You can't have both veg and lots of good brown gravy".

Now, on rare occasions, if the roast was left alone . . . not forced to share its room with vegetables . . . not like me and my brothers, them sleeping on a bunk bed and me on a cot, wedged in a tiny room meant to be a main-floor bathroom that never happened . . . no, if the roast was all alone in the pan, there'd be lots of dark brown drippings to make lots of gravy. Gravy to cover mashed potatoes, gravy to disguise over boiled canned peas already half hidden by lumps of gristle and yellow fat, gravy for Dad to sop up with a stack of bread.

Something to wipe off his plate, so that he could show us all how to use up everything and not waste anything.

And that lonely roast would give us gravy for tomorrow. Gravy to moisten the every-Monday-night, leftover roast beef diner. For the rare treat that Dad called shit-on-a-shingle; sliced meat on bread, smothered in gravy, served up with un-mashed boiled quarters of potato and another can of over cooked, mushy green peas.

But on this Sunday, when the roast leaves the table, and the big bowl of leftover potatoes and veg find a home in the round topped refrigerator, jammed into the crisper drawer or shoved to the back of the second shelf, up against a mug that is missing it's handle, a mug filled with saved layers of bacon grease for later fry-ups . . . .

Then we wait, silent, no kicking under the table, not looking at each other, afraid to see a gesture, or a stuck out tongue that might pull a squeak out of our throat, and start a fight, and make Mom angry and Dad demand punishment. We sit, stretching our ears to the kitchen, holding mid breath, praying to hear the words "Lick your forks kids, there's dessert."

## Cycling

You wanted a bike, now you've got a bike," Dad announces as he yanks a scratched and rattling collection of red and white metal out of the back of our family station wagon.

"But . . . ," I start, and then Dad cuts me off.

"Don't even start. This is a perfectly good bike for you to learn on." Dad picks it up, and then lets it drop and bounce on its huge wheels. The rattling noise is deafening. "A lady at work gave it to me to give to you. Isn't that nice? You should be grateful, right?"

"Yeah, Dad, sure," I say.

"I'll tell her you said thanks." Dad beams.

This is a full size woman's bike. It's 1960. I'm eight years old and short for my age.

"I'll fix it up, don't worry, it'll be fine. Steve will teach you how to ride," Dad says as he wheels the bike into our back yard and throws it onto the picnic table. With tools from the back shed, he lowers the seat and handlebars, checks the tires, oils the chain and then pronounces the bike ready for me.

My brother Steve agrees to go with me to the schoolyard across the road after dinner. Steve got a brand new, three-speed bike with hand brakes for passing last week. I think he feels a little bad about what I got.

Now, on the paved schoolyard, Steve holds the handlebar and the seat post and tells me to get up on the seat. I manage to climb up and sit, but even with my legs extended, my toes still dangle at least four inches above the pedals.

"You're gonna have to learn to ride standing up," Steve tells me. "Stand on the pedals."

I lower myself off the seat to get my feet onto the pedals. My shoulders are almost touching my ears when I hold the handlebar.

"Okay, I'll hold onto the back of the bike. You start pedalling."

I pedal, trying to keep the bike upright and aimed straight. Steve lets go. The bike and I fall down.

We continue like this for ten minutes. That is the extent of Steve's guilt motivation. The lesson is over, and we go home.

OVER THE NEXT WEEK I try to ride daily. Soon I can balance myself like I'm on a scooter. I push off and glide, but every time I try to stand and pedal, I fall. The next week, the bike only comes out of the shed once or twice.

All my friends ride bikes. The schoolyard swarms with kids on brand new, kid-sized bikes all day and into the evening, until the street lights come on and we all have to get back home.

Now it's the middle of August, and I haven't tried riding for more than three weeks. I get the bike from the shed and wheel it to the schoolyard where there are six other kids circling and weaving around each other. I get over near the fence by the grass and step onto the pedals. I push off, tip over, stop, push off, tip over, stop. Then Kevin Simpson swoops by. He's my friend Donna's five-year-old brother. He laughs and yells, "You're eight and you can't ride!"

I stand up on the pedals, push off, then pedal, and pedal, and pedal again and again and again.

NOW I'M EIGHTEEN AND LIVING the hippie lifestyle with my boyfriend in a ten-dollar-a-week, seven-by-ten foot room, on Church Street in Toronto.

John gets casual day work with Help Unlimited. He nets maybe six or seven dollars a day based on the $1.05 an hour minimum wage in 1970. I get a job delivering orders on foot for a restaurant on Yorkville Avenue for a flat rate of $30.00 a week.

The first Saturday after I get the job, I'm on my own while John is working. I stop by the Trailer, a drop-in for street youth. It has moved into a basement, two doors west of the restaurant, but kept the name from when it was actually located in a trailer.

There's a new counsellor there, Dave. He's a tall, skinny man with wispy, grey hair. He is a nervous guy with jerky movements. I don't see him lasting long. There are a few regulars at the drop in. I know them all and we sit talking for a while. Dave, just watches. Parked against the wall is a slim, dark blue bike. I get up from my chair and check it out.

"Who's bike?" I ask.

"Uh, it's mine," Dave says.

"Cool. Can I take it for a ride?" I ask.

"Uh, well, yeah, okay, but don't go far. It's all I have to get around on. You will bring it back, right?" Dave stutters.

"Yeah. Don't worry. I'll just go around the block," I say. "I haven't been on a bike in a few years; I just want to see if I can still ride."

"Oh," says Dave.

I ride west on Yorkville Avenue, south on Bay Street then east on Bloor Street. I'm doing okay. Turning left onto Yonge Street on a green, I decide to get the bike back to its owner before he gets sweaty. Just above Bloor, I check behind me. Northbound traffic is still on a red light. I peddle a bit more, signal my intention to turn left onto Cumberland and lean into the turn.

Bang!

I fly off the bike and onto the road. I am on the ground. The bike is between me and a big, black Ford LTD with a long scrape down the passenger side. A lady gets out of the car and comes over to look down at me.

"I have to get my daughter to her hairdresser's appointment. You are going to make me late," she states.

I'm still on the ground when a cop appears.

"You okay?" he asks.

"My leg hurts, but I think it's okay," I say.

I get up and tell him what happened. I signalled my intention to turn. She's got to be in trouble.

The cop pulls out his notebook and starts to write. "Actually," he says, "You were just about to turn into Cumberland Street. It is a one-way street and you were heading the wrong way. You may very well have to pay for the damage to her car," he says without looking up.

The driver looks at me and smirks.

I cannot afford this.

I lean against a nearby lamppost, hold my abdomen and look at the cop and the driver.

"I hope I don't lose the baby," I say.

The driver huffs, she and the cop talk for a minute, then they both drive off.

I wheel the bike back to the drop-in. It's okay, but I suffer great pain every day for a month, delivering lunches on a sprained left ankle.

I am determined to never ride a bike again.

FORTY-THREE YEARS LATER, I'VE JUST moved to Hamilton. Living down in the city's east end, I realize a bike may be a good option for transportation because I don't have a car.

So, I get my son to help me pick out a bike. I get a Biria. It's big, black, sturdy, and has a low step-over. It takes a year and a half, but I figure out the hand brakes and gears. I look silly in a lime green helmet, terrified, jerky and slow, but I'm on the road and riding.

In my second summer of cycling, on August 24th, 2014, I decide to ride to Dundas and back, twenty kilometers. I take Cannon Street, and ride in the north lane. At Hughson I stop for a red light. Resting my foot on the curb, I wait for the light to change, check for traffic behind me, and then push off when the light turns green. I move into the lane.

Bang!

And I'm on the ground looking at a silver, hatch back that has stopped just ahead of me, then I watch the car pull away and disappear.

A man walking across the street stops, helps me and my bike up, picks up my back-pack and cell phone and hands them to me, then he leaves.

Now I'm on the sidewalk with a bloody left elbow. It's scraped badly and looks gruesome. My bike is okay.

And I'm angry . . . blazing angry. Some asshole has hit me, taken off, and worse, has made me face the question again. Should I ride a bike or not. I'm already thinking of wording for an on-line ad to sell my bike.

I feel defeated and vulnerable.

I feel old.

Now, another man is walking toward me on the sidewalk. He asks if I'm okay. I tell him in angry sobs that an idiot hit me with his car then took off.

He's staring at my torn elbow. "That was me," he declares. "But you hit me."

"What!" I yell.

"Yeah, you hit me," he says again.

"I have a right to be in a lane!" I start yelling back at him, three, maybe five times. Then I wheel my bike away from him and over to James Street to the Mulberry coffee shop.

I call my son. He meets me, we clean up my elbow, and he listens to my anger, frustration and fear.

Then I finish my coffee and get back onto my bike and ride to Dundas and back.

Less than three weeks later bike lanes open on Cannon Street.

# RITA BAILEY

*Rita Bailey writes short memoir, opinion pieces, what she calls "bad" poetry and gardening articles while she labours away at a murder mystery set in post-World War I, Toronto.*

## CRIMINALS AND OTHER RIFFRAFF

I hesitate, reluctant to sit. But my husband, Paul, has already placed two steaming mugs on the table across from a shaggy-haired man who looks like a miniature Hagrid.

Paul pats the seat beside him. "Sit down, meet my buddy Sam."

Sam nods a greeting. I force a wooden smile, not in the mood for small talk. We're on our way to the hospital across the street, where Paul's best friend, Carl, is on life support. Conflicting emotions churn my stomach. Guilt because I've been away, leaving Paul to make this daily trek on his own. Dread, as I imagine what awaits us: whispered voices, machines pumping with mindless efficiency, and Carl—or the hollow shell that used to be Carl. But Paul needs a distraction, so I sit and take a sip of coffee. Dark and slightly bitter.

Sam holds up his cell phone.

"Wanna see my cats?" he asks. Three cute kittens pop into view on the screen. They peek cautiously from behind a heap of rotting boards and rusty paint cans in what looks like an alley. From the corner of the screen a hand appears, holding a bowl of food. The kittens squeal and scamper toward it, leaping over each other in their hurry. I laugh in spite of myself.

"Someone just dumped them," Sam says. "Like they were garbage. They're crazy for Tuna Pate but The Dollar Store was all out, so I got Chicken 'N Gravy instead."

That must cost a fortune." Paul reaches into his pocket. "Can we give you a donation?" We both have a soft spot for cats.

"Naw, don't worry about it." Sam waves the money away. "I don't pay for the stuff. I boost it from The Dollar Store."

"Have you ever been caught?" Paul asks.

Sam looks insulted. "No way, man. When they get wise to me, I move on. There's no shortage of dollar stores in this city."

"Sort of like the Robin Hood of cats," I say.

"Robin Hood." Sam ponders the title. "Yeah, that's what I am."

We say goodbye and cross the street to the General. Cigarette butts line the sidewalk like tubular confetti, and the garbage can by the entrance overflows with coffee cups.

Once inside, Paul navigates the maze of corridors to the CCU. The atmosphere is hushed, like church, the only sound the squeak of our shoes. After a succession of lefts and rights that I'll never remember on my own, we arrive at Carl's cubicle. Tubes snake in and out of his body and there's a soft hiss as his chest rises and falls with the help of a respirator.

I swallow the lump in my throat and pull up a chair next to Paul. Our conversation rambles: Sam and his kittens, Trump's latest tweet, the fortunes of the Leafs. We tell him we're caring for Kato, his eighteen-year-old tabby. We don't tell him that she spends her day curled up on one of his old shirts, her face buried in her paws.

The window ledge is lined with pictures and mementoes Paul brought from Carl's apartment. We thumb through his high school yearbooks.

"Hey Carl, how did you get the nickname Rowdy?" Paul asks. The Carl we know is about as rowdy as a plate of liver and onions.

"Who's this Nancy who signed your yearbook 'with lots of love'"?

"You made the senior boys' basketball team?"

We talk as if we expect Carl to sit up and answer, but the only response we get is the occasional beep of a monitor. Carl doesn't have any family, no one to make a decision. Next week Paul will meet with the doctors and a lawyer and a guy from the Ministry of Whatever and decide who has the authority to pull the plug. When that happens it's a matter of time. Minutes, they tell us. The stroke has done too much damage. There is no chance of recovery.

I stare at the graphs that zigzag across one of the machines, the one that records Carl's breathing, pulse and blood pressure. His heart is strong.

Paul met Carl at a karate dojo some thirty-odd years ago. Before Carl's stroke they practiced their punches and kicks at a club every Monday night. Recently, they added a new hobby: people watching at coffee shops around the city. Each venue has a code name: The Criminal Cafe, The Great Mall of China, Biker City Coffee.

Maybe that's why Paul heads for the coffee shop across the street on every visit. It's a ritual. Almost as if he expects to see Carl sitting there, waiting for him.

Later that week, before another hospital visit, we meet Sam again. He shows us a clip from an old *Columbo* episode on his phone. Called "Candidate for Crime," it's about a politician who kills his campaign manager. We watch the shabby detective slouch around a tailor shop, fingering the expensive material, while the snooty owner looks on, horrified. It's classic *Columbo*, the little guy standing up to the power brokers. We tell Carl about it and I swear his eyes blink in approval.

As we're driving home, Paul fills me in about Sam.

"He rents a room around here, has some creative ways to stretch his budget."

"Such as?"

"There's the empty pop bottle trick. He goes into a fast food place right at shift change. Fills it up when no one's looking."

"All that sugar can't be good for him."

"He walks it off hiking around town, looking for places to rip off," Paul counters. "You know those plastic keys that open toilet paper dispensers in public washrooms? He's got one. Free toilet paper for life. Then there's the dumpster diving. Apparently grocery stores throw out all kinds of good stuff. Tzatziki dips, Sriracha sauce, organic yoghurt. One day past their expiry date."

"So what's his story?" I say. "Why is he scrounging around dumpsters?"

Paul pulls into our driveway. "Sam did some time. It's hard to get a job with a record." He looks at me to gauge my reaction.

"Oh," I say. "So we're hanging out with criminals now."

"He feeds stray cats."

"With stolen food."

Paul shrugs. "The man has standards. He only steals from the Big Guys."

He has a point.

As our hospital trips fall into a familiar routine, I actually find myself looking forward to our meetings with Sam.

A few days later, Paul puts on his best shirt and a tie and heads to the big meeting, the one that will release Carl from this artificial purgatory. I sit in the waiting room, pretending to read; jerking my head up every time the door whooshes open.

"What happened?" I ask when he finally appears. I can't read his expression.

"The lawyer stalled for time, said he needs another week to do due diligence."

"What does that mean?" I ask.

"It's called gaming the system. Why get paid for one meeting when you can get paid for two?" His voice is as cold and hard as a blade.

What it means for Carl is another week lingering in a place he no longer belongs. His breathing is laboured now, his skin grey. His arms are starting to swell. "That happens at this stage," the nurse says. "His kidneys are failing."

Carl's cat, Kato, is shutting down, too. She refuses food, turns her head away when I try to give her water through a dropper. She smells like something rotting. I stroke her matted fur and thank her for being Carl's sidekick all these years. Tears that I've held back for days drip down my face.

A week later, Paul attends the second meeting. This time I stay with Carl. I flip through the photo albums on the window ledge and pause at a picture of him sitting on Santa's knee. He looks about five, dressed in a plaid shirt, his hair slicked down. I hope he got whatever it was he asked for.

Paul comes back, his mouth a thin line. "This time the lawyer brought his own lawyer. Some relative. Can you imagine the bill for that? The suits get all the gravy." He lets out a long breath. "But we reached a decision. They'll take Carl off life support sometime today."

We don't say much as we cross the street to the coffee shop. There, Sam grouches about his landlord.

"Man, you should see the losers he rents to. I swear the guy downstairs is dealing crack. There's people coming and going at all hours. I told my landlord he's got to be more selective, stop renting to riffraff."

I smile at the irony. Later, as we cross the parking lot to our car, I think about how we label people. Sam steals cat food and gets branded a criminal; a lawyer rips off the system and gets a handshake, a pat on the back. Who is the real criminal and who gets to decide?

We're only home a few minutes when the hospital calls. They're ready to remove the tubes; does Paul want to be there? He hurries back out the door.

I sit on the floor with Kato and reach into my pocket for a tissue to wipe my eyes. Instead my fingers close around a smooth square—Carl's picture with Santa. Somehow I'd pocketed it earlier. I stare into Carl's eyes. They're wide open, looking straight at the camera, scared and brave at the same time.

# DEAN CARRIERRE

*Dean Carrierre wrote the best-selling book* Solar House for a Cold Climate *in 1979 and hasn't attempted to have anything published since, though he has done a lot of scribbling in the interim. He writes poetry and prose on subjects as wide ranging as the environment, human justice, ant farmers, talking-walking fish . . . whatever strikes his fancy. His imagination knows no bounds, though many have argued there should be. His latest piece is entitled "Two Fleas On A Chicken . . . A Love Story."*

*He attempts to live following Gandhi's advice, "Live simply, so that others may simply live."*

## THE RED SHOES

Sami was home-birthed to Assim and his wife Fatima, in their modest block bungalow on the outskirts of Juba, the capital of South Sudan. Fatima ran a one-woman sewing shop in a wood-framed, steel-roofed lean-to attached to the side of their house. Assim hadn't been able to work in the carpet mill since he'd lost his left arm to a machete wielding rebel during the war. He helped around the house, looked after Sami and became very adept at getting the best deals at the market place. Thus they were able to have a simple but happy life.

Sami's parents noted early on that he was possessed of an unusual combination of intelligence, curiosity and strength. They let him crawl, climb and explore everywhere. As he developed, they introduced him to many things and people in the community: the rhythmic poetry of the blind woman at the market, the guitarist who played for change outside the corner grocery store, the dancers in the neighborhood park.

As Sami learned to walk, Assim played a game whereby Sami would score by kicking a small ball between two milk jugs set up as goal posts against the back wall of the house. Assim and Sami had so much fun trying to score on each other that often they would roll on the soft ground with laughter.

When Sami grew older Assim took him to the local playing field to join other young soccer players. It soon became evident that Sami had unusual gifts. He was always the best player in his age group. Not only was he a good scorer but he was a good team player. He had an uncanny ability to not only know where every player was at all times but to anticipate where players would be in the moments ahead. By the time Sami was fourteen he had broken every record in every division where he played.

Not only was Sami excelling at soccer, he was displaying exceptional academic ability. It was suggested that he go to one of the country's elite schools. Some schools and soccer clubs from other countries even began to take notice. Sami was not interested even though he had all the confidence to handle the pressures of being away from home. Sami loved his life, he loved his friends . . . and he wasn't moving.

The day after Sami won the under-sixteen scoring title Assim and Fatima presented him with a pair of shiny, bright red soccer shoes. Sami was thrilled beyond words. That afternoon he donned his new shoes and went for his usual six kilometer run to the next village. As he sped along the dirt road, he felt as though he was gliding above the roads surface. He was so happy . . . .

Several days later when he awoke in the hospital, his left arm, chest and head were covered with bandages. His lower body was covered with a white sheet. He opened his eyes to see a pretty young nurse in a crisp, white-and-blue uniform standing beside his bed. He recognized her as the one who had given him a vaccination at school.

"Where are my red shoes?" Sami asked.

Tears started to roll down the nurse's face. She stammered, "Sami . . . you have no shoes . . . You have no feet. You stepped on a land mine."

# A Tale of Two Trees

In Bayfront Park a lone, young maple, half-dressed in autumn shades of green and brown is rooted on a small knoll. The base of her trunk is ringed by a thick blanket of yellow leaves and a broader field of green grass. She stands against a bright blue sky . . . a sky where two jet contrails are painted a brilliant gold by the setting sun.

The tree stands bursting with youthful optimism. Though fixed in place, she travels in time . . . with the old couple in matching electric wheel chairs holding hands as they motor side-by-side through the park . . . with the Hindu wedding party dancing under the trees . . . with the seagulls sailing on the wind.

To her and many more this is the land of hope.

MEANWHILE IN YEMEN, A DRAGON BLOOD tree weeps. She has stood rooted in the stingy soil for over two thousand years. Old men have played chess and debated village affairs under her boughs. Children climbed into her branches and sang. Farmers harvest her berries to feed to their cows and sheep. Cinnabar, its red resin, has been used in a wide range of medicines. Her dye, "dragons blood," is thought to have been responsible for the intense color of Stradivarius violins.

Now she stands witness to Saudi Arabian Boeing F-15 Eagle fighter jets flying overhead supported by United States reconnaissance and aerial refueling aircraft. In the course of these bombing raids many civilians have been killed in addition to fighters. Schools and hospitals have been destroyed. The only shipping port has been bombed, making it very difficult to deliver humanitarian aid. This has the potential to be the biggest humanitarian crisis of recent times.

So the dragon tree weeps and wonders. She wonders if there will ever be an end to war.

# SHANNON CHARTRAND

*Shannon's day job was Marketing Research Manager at Purina Nestle. After retirement, she began taking writing courses and is enjoying writing short vignettes.*

## THE HAND YOU'RE DEALT

We're rehashing today's baseball game while wolfing down grilled hot dogs and Cokes in front of old lady Bracken's store. We beat Pinehurst for the first time all summer, so the bragging is over the top: "They never saw it coming!" "Teach them a lesson!" "Don't mess with East Greenfield!"

I see one of my brothers heading towards us. He's on a mission, head down, walking fast. "You're not going back to school. You're getting a job," he blurts out as he reaches me.

"Who says?" I challenge.

"Who do you think, asshole? Mom and Dad."

"Lucky bugger!" mumbles Malcolm, whose dad is serving time in Kingston Pen for armed robbery. Even his father knows the value of an education. It's the Fifties. Kids need high school now.

I fling my half-eaten hot dog into the steel barrel and tear home. Pleading with my parents, I say, "I like school, Dad, and two of my brothers are working. Why can't I stay in school?"

"You don't need high school to do manual labour," Dad reasons.

"If I go to high school, I won't have to do manual labour," I say.

Dad laughs, "Going to be a brain surgeon, are we? Who do you think you are? You're getting a job."

My face burns with shame.

I get a job at Brossard's Grocery, stocking shelves, sweeping floors and stuff. I don't mind the work. The boss is happy. What hurts is when I see Malcolm and the guys walking to school, but I'll get used to it. Malcolm always waves, hand high above his head.

By January, Dad has found me a better paying job in a woodworking shop.

AT FIRST LIGHT, I EMBARK in a blizzard, on a two-hour journey, mostly on foot, to a job I don't want. I hunker down in my father's short, army coat. The bitter cold seeps through the woollen coat and the weight of Dad's boots exhausts me. How did the Allies win the war in this gear? Snow drifts impede my every step. Bitter winds, laden with snow sting my face.

In the next town, I meet up with Wally, Dad's acquaintance. He takes me on a long, bus ride to his woodworking shop. The bus is a mobile block of ice and snow. Windshield wipers up-front provide the only outside view.

At the shop, I relax into its warmth. As feeling returns, my skin tingles and burns. Feeling starts as pins and needle sensations in my fingers and toes. The pungent smell of the forest arouses memories of playing Cowboys and Indians, climbing trees and building teepees. I feel a sense of longing, for what, I don't know.

Wally demonstrates how to saw the lumber. He flicks on the electric blade and there is a shrill, drum-piercing, whirring sound. He guides the wood towards the menacing blade, shearing it in half like curtains opening.

Then it is my turn. I am terrified but desperate to impress Wally, a former army private. I slide my board towards the blade, expecting the jagged teeth to chew through the wood with ease. Instead, the saw hits a knot in the wood. The board bounces upward, flinging my hand into the sinister blade. I hear four discreet sounds:

Ping . . . ping . . . ping . . . ping.

Instinctively, I know it's the sound of steel cutting bone. This is the hard way to learn that electric saws cannot cut through knots.

No ambulance will get through until the roads are ploughed. Wally springs into action. He puts a tourniquet on my forearm and plunges my hand into a jute bag of sawdust to absorb the blood. We set out on foot for the bridge to Montreal. I plod in Wally's footsteps through the heavy snow. My crimson forearm is bent skyward like an Olympic torch. Scarlet globs of blood mar the snow behind me in Hansel and Gretel fashion.

What are the odds we stumble upon a doctor's house? I'd say pretty slim. But there's the sign. Wally pounds on the door. A short, stumpy woman answers in her housecoat. "The doctor is too drunk to see you," she says in a matter of fact voice as though announcing he's in surgery. Something plummets inside me . . . a sinking feeling . . . maybe fear, anger, I don't know. Between my father and this pathetic excuse for a doctor, I figure alcohol will be the death of me.

As we reach the bridge, a car stops alongside us. The doctor's wife has called an off-duty policeman. My gratitude is unbounded. The driver hands me a map to save his upholstery. He shifts the gears into drive. We hear the futile squeal of tires spinning as the car sinks gently into the snow. Wally and I get out and rock the rear bumper until the tires gain traction. We hop in and zigzag across the bridge, towards the hospital.

I awaken to the sound of metal scraping on metal. An orderly is stealing bus change from my night table. Why not, I figure. It's been the worst day of my fourteen years. At least I'm warm now. My right hand is smothered in white gauze, punctuated by a jagged, red stain. I want to cry but can't. If my parents were here, I could stop being brave.

A young doctor enters my room, "You've had a bad accident, son, but you are going to be okay. Your thumb and three fingers were severed. I evened them above the knuckles. Your parents have been notified."

My pinky has been spared. I am horrified at the extent of my loss. It is hard to be grateful for stumps. I want my fingers back. I want to catch a baseball. Most of all, I want to go to school.

Once I am released from the hospital, I make my way home by bus. Mom and I sit on the couch. All the other kids have disappeared except for five-year-old Shannon who peaks around the door frame. Mom speaks softly, "I know, Son, you've had a bad accident. Of course, you're sad. Cry until you have no more tears." She pats my back. "The doctor called on Dockerel's phone. I ran over there to speak to him. He tells me you are going to be fine. You will learn to use your damaged hand as well as you used it before the accident. He says you showed amazing courage getting to the hospital. That same courage will get you through this very hard part of your life."

Dad arrives late at night in a taxi, probably with a flask of gin in his pocket. He reaches up to the top bunk and pats my back beneath the army coat. His touch makes my skin crawl. He says "I'm sorry, Son." I pretend I'm asleep.

"Insurance money is blood money," says Dad, and he wants no part of it. He's too proud for that. So, I face the insurance board alone. Picture me, fourteen, scrawny, wearing my father's army boots in the dog days of summer, sitting alone in front of a long table with three, well-fed men in dark suits and ties on the other side. At the end of the table, a pretty, young secretary sits to the left of her boss, taking shorthand. Her boss is rubbing her calf with his stockinged foot.

They ask me how I've been managing since the accident. I say I'm doing well with stubs for fingers, explaining all the daily tasks I've mastered like tying my shoes and getting dressed. It doesn't occur to me to say what I can no longer do.

"Our company will compensate you for your loss for the rest of your life. Of course, it will be the minimum amount since the loss of your fingers has not resulted in much hardship," says the portly one. He could be saying "my company is going to screw you out of a lot of money" but because he's smiling, I smile back. No offence given. No offence taken. In addition, they offer me a job at the wood shop where I lost my fingers. I shake my head, no.

My first insurance cheque arrives in the mail. I tuck it into my jeans pocket to cash in town on my lunch hour. Dad shows up in the lobby of my shop around 1:00 p.m. He "needs" my insurance money.

## STILL ON THE GREEN SIDE

I s now a good time, Dad?" I ask. He's looking more and more shrivelled in his large bed. There's an antiseptic smell in the room, like a swimming pool. Mom has been sterilizing everything in sight as if that could ward off death.

"Come in, Son, while I'm still on the green side," says Dad.

A list of his meagre investments lies by his lamp. He's leaving Mom the house plus $10,000 in investments. It was hard to save that much money. He's trying to make amends; do the right thing.

I sink into the lumpy chair beside his bed. "We have to talk," he says. The effort to speak sets him coughing. His lungs are getting weaker. I hold a glass of cognac to his lips. He takes a sip.

Dad quit drinking ten years ago but asked for Hennessy Cognac now to help him sleep. Our surname is Hennessy, but we seem to have fallen off the family tree.

Dad and I creep across the room to the window. I slide it wide open. It's March with a dollop of May. Sunshine caresses our faces. Fresh, cool air wafts in. Dad says, "I don't want to die." He yearns for one more spring. I squeeze his shoulder and pull him closer. "Too painful to live. Too painful to die," he says. I get him back to bed.

"It's time to push me out to sea on an ice floe," he says.

37

This is in reference to a family joke.

"That's not funny," I say.

"You kids used to think it was hilarious," he says. "You'd collapse helplessly in mirth at the thought of me floating into the sunset on a hunk of ice."

"We meant it in a nice way, Dad. You have to admit, it did cheer you up," I say.

We are joined by an old friend, Ben.

"My dear friend," says Dad, "thank you for coming. I have fond memories of our Friday nights years ago. Once we were half in the bag, we'd belt out the song 'Goodnight, Irene' over and over until the neighbours begged for mercy."

Ben asks, "Do you remember the silly song we sang for our kids?

*Mairzy doats and dozy doats and liddle lamzy divey*
*A kiddley divey too, wouldn't you?*

To my amazement, Dad sings along with Ben.

Once Dad has had some rest, I prop him up and lather his face for shaving. An audiobook of *Huckleberry Finn* is playing. It's a favourite from his youth. As I carefully shave the contours of his face, an image of myself as a boy watching Dad shave comes to mind. Shaving was one of the portals into manhood which fascinated me. Now, it is a portal into death which saddens me. Halfway through shaving, Dad signals he's had enough. I wipe the lather from his face and position him for sleep.

"Make arrangements with the doctor," he mutters.

Downstairs, Mom sits on the couch, staring at the floor. Her arms cradle her chest. She looks up and says, "He asked me if I love him. I said 'no'. Should I have said 'yes'?"

Words fail me. I know she loves him.

Darkness comes early this time of year. It seems appropriate to do these things under the cloak of night. The bedside lamps glow dimly. The doctor is in attendance. My seven siblings have joined me. Someone is sniffling. Mom holds Dad's hand. She tells him he's the only man she ever loved, even through the hard times.

"I know, Jess. I wish I had treated you better," he says.

Each of us tells Dad why we love him. Dad says, "Do you know what I wish for all of you . . . I wish you sons and daughters exactly like you. I have been a very fortunate man."

Our eldest sister enters, carrying a cake, sparklers blazing. I say, "Dad, I know your preference was to die in the dining room of a cruise ship immediately after eating Baked Alaska. Couldn't get you on a cruise ship but here's the Baked Alaska."

"You guys are nuts," says Dad, smiling.

Dad has requested we play "I'll Be Seeing You" by Vera Lynn. She was the allied soldiers' sweetheart during World War II. The doctor is to administer the lethal dosage when the song ends.

Dad's breath diminishes to the vanishing point. His suffering is over. So, too, are his spring times.

# LINDA CHRISTOFF

*Linda Christoff lives in Hamilton where she volunteers with*
*many community groups. She writes, draws and knits for fun.*

## GRANDMA

U s children got a surprise, which we didn't know we
were going to get at the time. Our parents never talked
about my Dad's parents at all, and us children thought they
were dead. So we never asked any questions about them.

It was late afternoon when my Mother got the call saying
some of my Dad's family would show up later that evening,
when we got introduced to them.

I had thought my Dad was an only child. To find out he
had siblings shocked me. My Mom served them tea and coffee
in the kitchen, so us children could watch our TV programs,
and they had privacy so they could talk.

We knew when each show was over, the youngest should
go to bed. When only my brother and I were left, we figured

we would find out what was happening, but we were told to go to bed early that evening. I wasn't tired so I stayed awake so I could find out what was going on.

My parents were fighting with Dad's family, but I couldn't hear everything. From what I did hear, I figured someone was going to stay with us, but I didn't know who or for how long.

Dad's family left and my parents went to bed, but they were still fighting. Then I got very tired and drifted off to sleep without finding out who was coming.

THE NEXT DAY MY MOM was in a foul mood, so I kept my distance from her. That night, after I went to bed, I heard a car pull up, so I went to the window and looked out. There was a taxi, but it was so dark I couldn't tell if it was a lady or a man getting out. My parents were still outraged with each other, so I went right to bed and I fell asleep, but I knew that I would find out who this person was in the morning.

The next day the rest of the children woke up very early and I decided to read to them so they wouldn't cause any noise to wake that person up. I heard my Dad get up, and then my Mom, who told us to stay upstairs until she called us.

I wanted to meet this person so much that I thought my heart was going to explode. When my Mom called, I told the children to be quiet going downstairs. My brother asked, "who is it"? I told him that I didn't know, then he said again, "Do you know who it is?" So I told him what I had seen.

When I went downstairs, lying on the couch was an older woman. She was tiny and very slender, with gray hair. I couldn't help myself; I stood there staring at her.

Mom called me, so I went into the kitchen and Mom told me to be as quiet as a mouse. About twenty minutes went by, and then the lady came into the kitchen.

We were all staring at the lady when Mom told us to mind our own business. So we did, and Mom made breakfast for the lady. Then Mom told us to go and make our beds, and to get dressed, and to do our chores.

When we came back, the older lady had finished her breakfast and was dressed. Her hair was combed neatly and she had a bun on top of her head. I noticed that she must have braided her hair first before putting it into a bun.

Mom told us to come and sit down and then she told the lady our names. I looked straight into Mom's eyes saying, "What do we call her?"

Then Mom told us, "This lady is your grandmother."

I looked at her again saying, "That's not your mom".

Mom looked at me saying, "No, she's your dad's mom".

I opened my mouth to say something, but decided not to say anything. After a while, which was only a few minutes, Mom told us to go outside until lunch.

After lunch, Grandmother came outside and she had a red-and-white-checkered blanket over her right arm. All of us children were on the hill, under the evergreen tree, playing with dinky cars. As I looked at her, I realized she was looking up towards the sky. When I saw that, I knew that I really liked her. She spread out the blanket and took her shoes off, and lay down looking back at the sky.

I had the urge to speak to her, because I wanted to know more about her and Dad. So I went to her asking, "Why did I never meet you before? Do I have a grandfather also? What was Dad like when he was a child?"

She told me to slow down and she would try to answer my questions. She told me that my grandfather was a bad man, so it was better not to meet him.

When I asked, "Why was he a bad man"? Grandma told me to ask my parents, because she wasn't able to talk about it.

"Where have you and your family been" I asked?

She told me that some of them lived in the city, and some in the country as well as up north.

I asked about Dad again, and what was he like when he was a child?

She said, "He was quiet, and shy, but if he wanted something he would have it no matter what."

I don't know why, but I looked down at the blanket, and there on the blanket was a beautiful, sparkling red necklace. As I picked it up my grandmother grabbed it from my hand. I looked at her puzzled, and then she told me it was called a Rosary, which you use to say prayers in the Catholic faith.

"You must promise me that you will never tell your parents about it at all." So I said yes, I promise, and I never told anyone until now. Then I asked, "Why do you keep looking up into the sky?"

She told me that her mother got her to look up into the sky and to tell what shapes she could see in the clouds. I looked into her face wondering if she was joking. Then she pointed out a cloud and asked, "what shape does it look like?" I told her it looked like a lion's head, so she pointed out one that looked like a elephant's trunk. Then each one or two of the children kept coming over to see what we were doing. After a while all eight of us were lying looking up into the sky trying to find all the things in the clouds.

After a couple of hours of doing this, our grandmother said she was tired and had to go in because the sun was too much for her, so each of us children said our goodbyes.

When she went to grab her shoes, I got them first and I put them on her feet. I helped her to stand, then I kissed her on the cheek, and she smiled at me and kissed me on my forehead. That's when I felt very close to her.

Every day it was sunny, so Grandma would bring out her blanket and we would talk. About the fourth day I asked her what her first name was. She told me, it was Annie, and she was from Scotland. I asked her how old she was when she came here. She told me she was twenty-one and she met our grandfather on the ship and he swept her off her feet and they got married.

I asked, what was my grandpa's first name? She told me Samuel. She told me that Grandpa was from Ireland, so we are part Irish and Scottish as well. Plus what our mother's nationalities are.

Then my parents were invited to a BBQ Party, on the next Saturday night, so I was to watch the children while they went. Mom decided Grandma could help watch the children with me. Then the people who were having the BBQ insisted that Grandma come to the party also.

I was excited, because this meant I was the babysitter. I thought wow! my parents trusted me to watch the rest of the children! But then my parents kept taking turns calling every so often, asking if everything was okay. They didn't leave until the four youngest were asleep. That was around eight-thirty. So there was only us four older ones who were left watching the TV programs and we knew what time each of us had to go to bed. That night we got to watch what shows we liked before going to bed.

After my brother Barry went to bed, he fell asleep quickly, because he was very tired from cutting three-quarters of an acre of hillside land that day.

When it was my turn to go to bed, I went to turn the TV off when an interesting movie came on. I didn't go to bed until two hours later, when the movie was over. I remember

Gregory Peck was in it. He was a newspaper guy who was persuing Audrey Hepburn who was a princess. They were in Rome, Italy, and the movie was called *A Roman Holiday*. Later in life I bought that movie and I even have it to this day.

Before they left for the BBQ party, Mom was saying to Dad, that she didn't want Grandma to go because she drinks too much and talks about the past.

It was after one in the morning and I couldn't sleep when I went to bed, so I just lay there.

Then I heard Mom screaming at my Dad, as they were walking along the village road.

I stood beside the window so I could hear, and see without being seen. I heard Dad say to Grandma to be quiet because everyone is sleeping. Dad had Grandma hanging on to him; she was walking then running as she tried to keep up. If he didn't have a hold of her she would have been on the ground.

Mom was walking very quickly ahead of them, screaming, "I told you she would ruin everything".

I heard the front door open and slam shut, so I tip-toed to my bed. Then I heard Dad yell at Mom to open the door.

She yelled back, "You promise to get rid of her tonight, or you can go with her!"

He screamed back, "Yes, just let us in so I can call a taxi."

Downstairs, Grandma was singing and falling all over the place. I could hear things falling and Mom saying stop her from banging into things and breaking them.

Then the taxi came and Dad helped Grandma to it. He sent Grandma away.

That was the first time I had ever seen a person drunk. I was so upset that Mom had Grandma sent away. I cried myself to sleep that night. I felt like I lost her forever.

The next morning, the rest of children asked, "Where did she go?" Mom just said, "she had to go back home."

I never saw her again, because she died four days before my thirteenth birthday and was buried on my birthday. No cake, no party. I had to babysit my brothers and sisters.

Even to this day I think of her, and I still love her.

# BERRY PICKING

When I was twelve years old, my brother told me about a strawberry-picking job just about a mile down the road from our home. I went to apply for the job and told the farmer that I had never picked berries before, but I was a fast learner. He showed me and I started; I wasn't scared of work then or now.

I must have been a good worker because he asked me to stay and pick blueberries next. Just picking strawberries I made almost $188.00 which in those days was lots of money.

I didn't last a full day picking blueberries, because the farmer found me passed out. He had the Volunteer Fire Department called. They took me to the hospital, who then called my mother.

I had an allergy to blueberries, which made my throat close up and I couldn't breathe at all. Mom called Dad at work and he came and got us. My parents told me that I could no longer work for the farmer, and I had to go and tell him.

The only thing I got from all my work was two pairs of walking shorts plus a red and white, short-sleeve top and runners for every day. My Mom told me the rest had to go on room and board. I really didn't understand so I thought that was unfair.

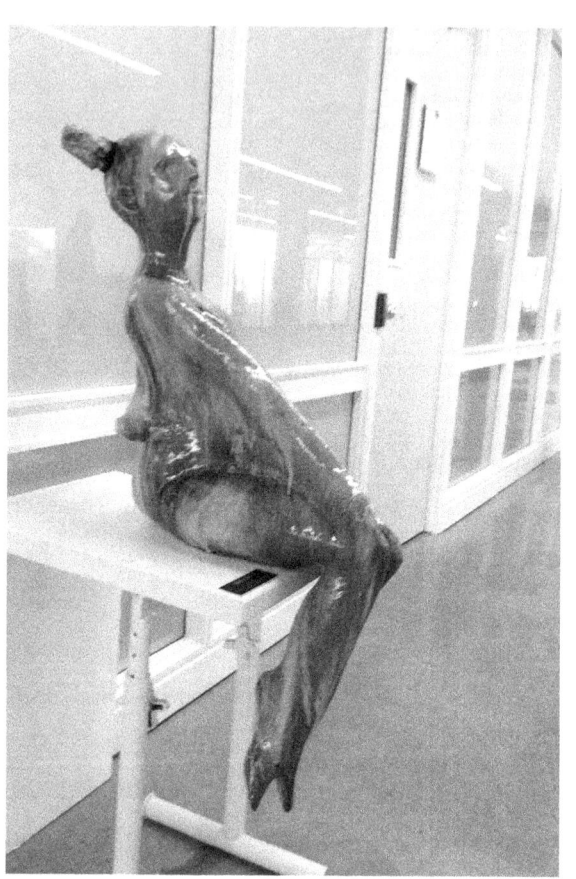

# CAROL FLEG

*My name is Carol Fleg. I started to write in a diary at age twelve and from there to a journal and now to stories and poetry about my family.*

## VOICES

As I sit in the food court of the local mall, the voices of many people can be heard. Some are loud; some are as low as a whisper.

The acoustics make it hard to distinguish one voice from the other. Deep voices heard from the men, higher from the women. Everyone sounds like they are talking at once.

As I look around at all the strangers, I can see their mouths moving, but have no idea what they are saying.

There are many different conversations on many subjects.

As the day comes to an end and the mall prepares to close for the evening, the voices become dimmer, almost to a whisper; there is no yelling because they can now hear one another.

As they leave the mall, the voices slowly fade as they walk away. Sitting there, when most have gone, the silence becomes very loud, and in the background I can hear the gates being closed and locks being turned.

My turn to leave; tomorrow is another day and all the voices will return once again.

# THE LITTLE PUPPY

Once upon a time—a long time ago . . .

There was a little puppy, who didn't know which way to go.

He looked to the left, then looked to the right.

He tried to avoid the big dog who wanted to fight.

He hid behind a tree

Hoping, if he saw the big dog, he would be able to flee.

The big dog was looking around,

But the puppy could not be found.

He searched, but to no avail,

He went around to the back of the house,

But did not even see nary a tail.

The little puppy came out from under the chair,

Looking for mom to protect him there.

He saw the big dog across the street.

So he quietly crawled to the door, his heart skipping a beat.

He cried at the door to get inside,

He waited for his mom to hear his cries.

He saw the door open and he ran for his life,

To the open paws of his mom, she comforted him and calmed his strife.

# A Tribute To My Friend

NEIL RICHARD TURNER

JULY 5, 1951 - AUGUST 1, 2017

We lived in the same apartment building: same address, different apartment number. A year ago we started having BBQ's. The cafe downstairs had closed and the tenants needed some way to purchase food on site.

It started slow and eventually picked up to three days a week. I helped out when they needed me.

One day, a man came up to me and ordered two cheeseburgers, but wanted them one at a time. He was an older gentleman, soft spoken, nice smile.

When I started going to the library to use their computers, he would be there, sitting in the food court just outside of the library. We always acknowledged each other. As time went on we had more conversations. He told me about wanting to become a priest. He explained that the teacher who was helping him with his studies had told him to go and talk to the head priest for the area churches, but that he should lie about his sexuality.

Neil was an honest man and wouldn't do it. Therefore he didn't get into the seminary to become a priest. He worked with his church, and with the seniors who were also members.

He knew my son and my son's partner, and so, eventually, we became friends. His sense of humour was priceless.

He liked his beer and on the way home from the mall he would stop at One Duke, for a couple. His friends would be there so he would have more then he should have. The next day he would tell me about his night at the bar.

He didn't talk much about his family, instead he talked mostly about the courses he wanted to take, but didn't always have the money for.

The last time I saw him was the last Saturday in July, 2017. He had his two cheeseburgers, one at a time. He seemed fine, maybe a little tired.

Monday, July 31st came, and I was doing the BBQ. He didn't come by for his two cheeseburgers, one at a time. I thought he was busy or had gone out of town for a few days.

He wasn't at the library, Monday, Tuesday or Wednesday.

I was worried by then and was going to ask someone to check on him. When I saw Gary, the head of our Social Committee, he told me the window cleaners had found him. He had suffered a heart attack and had been gone for at least a couple of days.

I was sad, but I knew he was at peace.

R.I.P., Neil, my friend.

# To My Children

When I spill some food on my nice, clean dress,
Or maybe forget to tie my shoe.
Please be patient and perhaps remember,
About the many hours I spent with you.
Then I taught you how to eat with care
Plus tying laces and your numbers too,
Dressing yourself and brushing your hair
Those were special hours spent with you.
So when I forget what I am about to say,
Just give me a minute or two,
It probably isn't important anyway.
And I would much rather listen just to you,
If I tell my story one more time,
And you the ending know through and through.
Please remember your nursery rhyme.
When I rehearsed it a hundred times with you,
When my legs are tired and it's hard to stand,
And walk the steady pace I would like to do.
Please take me carefully by the hand and guide me now,
As I so often did for you.

*Written by Bessie Culver, 1922- 2012*
*(Mother of Carol Fleg)*

# GLORIA GELLER

*In 2004, Gloria Geller retired with her life partner, Carolyn, to Hamilton, where she writes, weaves, practices yoga, and works in her garden.*

## THE HOUSE ON MILLWOOD ROAD

The house on Millwood Road was located immediately across from a school and conveniently close to a subway station in midtown Toronto. The owners rented the house to two professional career women in their forties, when the man of the house was transferred to Halifax to manage a branch of the bank he worked for. The renters, in their turn, advertised for someone to rent the third-floor attic. In my early twenties, and looking to rent my first very own apartment I was immediately drawn to the house and the attic apartment. I liked the slanted ceiling which gave the apartment a cozy feeling. There was a door leading to the attic which provided privacy, a kitchen at the top of the stairs, a separate bedroom as well as a living room, and I shared the second-floor bathroom with the two women.

I was very happy being in my very own apartment where I could play house, teach myself to cook, entertain if I wished, stay up most of the night to read and to write essays for the courses I was taking and just close the door and enjoy the solitude. Since I had a full-time job five mornings, three afternoons and a couple of evenings a week and attended university classes the other two nights, I was out of the house a good deal, so appreciated being able to enjoy the space when I could.

While friendly enough, my main contact with the two women in the house was on my way in or out when we would hold conversations about our activities and the events of the day. As I recall, they had nicely, but simply and comfortably furnished the house where they entertained friends around a large dining room table and where they spent evenings enjoying the comfortable chairs and couch in their sitting room. They also made use of the backyard, a place I don't ever recall seeing as they never suggested I might like to sit out in the back on those hot, sweaty summer days when the attic could be very steamy. On the other hand, I don't recall very often needing to escape the heat of the attic as I tolerated heat better back then.

I lived there for the better part of five years while working in downtown Toronto at an inner city settlement house that served low-income families and immigrants, many from Portugal; and working toward an undergraduate degree in sociology at Atkinson College, York University, at the north west corner of the city.

Very near to the end of my final school year I was told the homeowners were returning and the renters would be leaving. As I would be preparing for and writing my exams at the time this was to take place, I asked to remain in my apartment until my exams were over and the owners agreed.

The women left and an older couple returned; the old comfortable furniture left, replaced by new formal furniture. And with these changes someone or something stole the soul of the house; the warmth that had been there was replaced with a cold and empty feeling. The first time I walked down the flight of stairs from my apartment to the main floor of the house after the homeowners returned, I found myself enclosed in feelings of emptiness, loneliness, and isolation.

When a housecleaner arrived, the woman of the house watched as the other woman worked. I couldn't help but wonder why there was a need for someone else to clean the house when the owner seemed to have little to do except wait for her husband to come home. I don't know whether she left the house to meet with friends or had any other activities or interests, nor do I recall whether they had children and grandchildren visiting. I just know that the feel of the house changed drastically.

Unless I had experienced it, I would not have known how profoundly a house can be affected by the mere presence of different human beings, their belongings, their personalities, their relationships. Deeply affected by my observations, I walked around town looking at things differently, seeing beautiful homes as potential prisons for isolated and depressed women.

About ten years later, *The Women's Room,* a novel by Marilyn French describing the unhappiness of many middle-class housewives became a best seller. French's novel picked up on the same theme as *The Feminine Mystique,* an earlier book by Betty Friedan, who called the phenomenon the "problem that had no name." She too addressed the situation of middle class married women. It seemed to me they were describing the woman in this household. It was one thing to read about this phenomenon but another to be a witness to it.

The life lesson I gained from this experience was to be very grateful for the life I was living and to be very careful what I might wish for.

## Imprisoned in Amber

Ancient insect encased in amber, you
Fell from a shaky perch into a resin home,
Lay there for millennia within the coffin that
Enclosed, protected and embalmed you
In a permanent embrace, until one day
You were retrieved from your watery bed
By human hands.

I too fell from an insubstantial mourning perch
Became enclosed, protected and embalmed
Within the embrace of an amber cloak that held me fast
Until released by human hands and hearts.
I became free to run and dance
While you became a piece of jewellery
I wear around my neck.

## STREETSCAPE

Stars fade from the nightscape of the metropolis.

The poor, the homeless, ragged bundles of humanity,
    the only visible stars left in the urban firmament,
The mentally ill among them,
      burnt out remnants of life,
        whose light and energy
          once generated within a deep inner core,
        dim, collapse and
          disappear into a black hole.

# BEV JOSELIN

*Bev Joselin is a retired Speech Arts and Drama teacher . . . train-
ing that enabled many different occupations over a long career.
She now lives by the bay in Hamilton, Ontario, and is a happy
grandmother of seven ambitious Canadians.*

## THE BIG CHANGE

Thinking about chances taken could be remembering
times of fear. But of all the changes in my life, the most
significant was my move to Hamilton. Over many years there
were weekly trips from Toronto to Hamilton to pick up or
deliver students or children to day care, and later to rehearsals
and concerts. All these visits were to help and be with family.
So . . . on retirement the move made sense.

I thought: this will most likely be my last geographical
move . . . so it had better be right.

What did I leave?

A huge city, parts of which I have lived and worked in most of my life; places and friends known since childhood; involvement in many of the arts communities; membership in the cultural centres like the AGO and Ontario Museum and the activities involved there; the many, many theatres to attend.

Could I leave all that?

Why not?

It was only fifty-four miles away and there were my growing grandchildren with whom I would have time to spend.

THE FIRST CULTURE SHOCK CAME with my move to Dundas, where, twenty years ago, there were no Black or Asian faces or voices, although it was only fifty-four miles away from where I was used to seeing and hearing those thriving different cultures.

When I drove to Hamilton "proper" for a people fix, I found an apartment right by the water . . . just like the place where I was born and raised. The view over the harbour still sustains me after all these years.

It has been exciting to watch the rebirth of Hamilton from where I live at the harbour end of a thriving downtown . . . the constant changes on the main streets. The library is an anchor in many ways, serving all ages, interests and needs. As a choir "groupie," it's glorious to visit the many beautiful churches that are struggling to survive.

Volunteer positions have brought friends and learning opportunities. Most importanly, I enjoy the smaller city attitude. The generosity of people speaking to you on the street, at bus stops, even on the bus. It is certainly not the same experience in the BIG CITY . . . where nobody has time.

When I return to Hamilton after a visit to Toronto, I am still surprised by the gentler sounds on the street and, when I reach my home, feeling the breezes off the water, just as it was at Scarborough Bluffs and the Beaches in my past.

And those grandchildren? Well they are now all employed or at college or university.

Thank you, Hamilton. Change can be a wonderful gift.

## Bus Life in Hamilton

The difference between bus use in Toronto and in Hamilton was made very clear to me when I moved into my apartment. I had just given up my driver's licence—to my kid's delight—and heading out was a new adventure.

The first thing I noticed was how people conversed with you. Imagine the surprise this Torontonian experienced when after having been alerted by fellow riders that I had dropped a cucumber when getting ready to get off . . . and the driver said "get it and I will stop at the next block." That is when I started to say "thank you" when I got off the bus.

Now, at any of the six bus stops I use regularly, two to get to the city centre and four to return home, I meet familiar faces and, as we wait, we learn about each other.

Ken, who went to work on the same bus every day, shared his new marriage, then buying his first house and later we learned of his coming fatherhood. Since then, I have met him on the street with that child who is now six years old.

Rita asked me at the bus stop one morning if she could bring her resume for me to deliver to a workplace for her. When she came to my apartment, we found that we had mutual friends in the Toronto Literacy Organization where we had both worked in the past.

Emma was a very interested lady when she learned that I was headed to the library to learn about writing. She announced that she was a published writer of things occult, and how far and often she had to go to attend conferences. That gave several of us food for thought on the trip.

Susan I meet every Friday morning, as she is on her way to Burlington. She is a potter and is very busy making pieces for shows all over the GTA. She also travels a great deal and has good stories to tell.

One Friday, waiting at the stop across from the Market, I met a fellow who was going back to the ships after getting the passport that would enable him to go to the United States. He was from Newfoundland and was delighted with Hamilton and to find a craft beer store very near his ship's dock.

Every trip is different and many are a surprise. Like the time two elderly ladies sized me up and then invited me to go with them to a seniors' exercise class they were heading to.

And then there is my cheese lady. She and her son are the vendors opposite the elevator in the Market. She has taught me a great deal about cheese as we wait in the cold or rain.

I miss the convenience of driving but have much more fun on the bus. So carry on HSR . . . and it doesn't hurt that riders get a free pass at eighty.

## Free Time

Those of us over sixty may find that free time is not a positive part of one's life. When you were young, so many influences guided your days . . . religion gave hard rules to live by, parental power set other rules to live by, and then school dictated your use of time to secure your future.

So, when you reached adulthood the habits were set . . . get to work on time, work hard and then fill your time with personal and community advances and advantages.

Now, those habits are very hard to break . . . keep an orderly household, see to family needs, retain friendships and turn up when and where expected.

However, with the realization that some of the above needs seem to be set in stone, we *can* exercise our free will and therefore free time . . . but it takes practice.

One can find that late at night the imagination can lead you to relax and enjoy all sorts of activities that don't involve a meal to be prepared, a floor to be vacuumed, a phone call to make or an appointment to be kept. For me, the place to escape from busyness is in music. Just to listen, hear and feel the freedom of harmony, rhythm and physical vibrations. So, move to it, rest in it, use it like a hot shower and enjoy unguided and unrequired results.

THAT is free time!

# DARYLE LEFLER

*Born in Brampton, Ontario, Daryle E. Lefler grew up in Hamilton. "DE" taught in the primary grades for a couple of years. Now retired from H&R Block, DE indulges in plein air painting, fiction and poetry writing and a wide variety of handcrafts.*

## PERCEPTION

I'd heard so much about the new painting acquired by the city art gallery. The critics were raving. Art lovers were flocking in the thousands to exclaim excited praise for this new wonder of the art world. I had to go and see this treasure for myself. I mean, it must be pretty darn spectacular to cause all this fuss, right?

So, now I stand and stare at a huge, white canvas hanging in the place of honour at the Royal Art Gallery. A blue dot above the middle on the left, a red dot nearer to top on the right, both floating in a sea of white.

I've viewed it from a distance, now I get up close and personal. I can see haphazard brush strokes but can find no hidden artistic creations, like in those paintings that seem to be of a person, but on closer examination one finds many other forms making up the whole. Not so here. I back up. Nope. Just two dots and white paint. Seriously? They paid a million dollars for this nonsense.

"My five-year-old granddaughter did something better last Tuesday," I mutter.

"Isn't it outstanding? Doesn't it just punch you in the gut?"

I turn to eye the lanky youth who now stands beside me. I had thought he was being sarcastic, but no; I can see by the reverence on his face that he meant both astonishing statements.

"Oh come now! You can't really see anything here but two dots and a lot of nothing," I say, slashing my arm towards the painting.

The young man's blue eyes widen. "NO NO, look! Look at the brush strokes. See how angry and choppy they are on the right where the grey fog rages and Anger is supreme," he said in rising excitement, indicating the red dot. "But here, on this side, the white is misty; the strokes are gentle swirls, as Hope, the blue sphere, rises, spreading light in this troubled world. It's just so powerful!"

I blink and take a closer look. Sure enough, the brush strokes were different and the white went from bright on the left to a bit darker on the right, but really, a million bucks? I shake my head, smile at the slashed-jean clad youth, and leave the youngster to his worship, as I head to the area that holds my favourite Rembrandt.

## COOING DOVES

The coo, coo cooing of the doves,
so beautiful the sound.
The poets write that this is so.
They rapturously weep.
But I bet my bottom dollar
They're not lured from tranquil sleep,
by coo, coo, cooing doves.

# BARBARA LEGIN

*Barbara Legin, born in Warsaw, Poland, came to Canada in
1962, via Italy, England and the United States.*

## THE LOST OMELETTE

Having spent too much time looking at fashions in the
stores along Oxford Street, which, as you know, is
in the centre of London, and having a long bus ride home,
Mother realized that there wouldn't be enough time for her
to prepare a proper dinner in time for my father's return from
work. She decided we'd have an omelette for dinner, and so
she bought some eggs from one of many street vendors, before
catching the Number 8 double-decker bus home.

Since there were no grocery stores in London's fashion dis-
trict many vendors would appear, illegally, every day around
lunch time and then again during evening rush hour, selling
a variety of goods like fruit in season, baked goods, eggs, etc.

In those days, 1958, there were no egg cartons. Eggs were sold by weight and gently deposited into a brown paper bag to be very, very carefully carried home.

It was the rush hour and the lower level of the bus was full. Mother had to climb the steep, metal stairs to the upper deck to find a seat. As she reached the top, the bus jerked violently as it started to move forward. Grabbing the railing with one hand to stop herself from falling backwards down the treacherous, spiral metal stairs, she lost control. The paper bag broke and all the eggs splattered onto the floor.

Regaining her balance, extremely embarrassed by the mess she had made, a little scared of receiving an unpleasant reprimand and regretting her loss, she quickly walked to an empty seat at the very front of the bus, and faked innocence.

Back then there were bus conductors on the buses, who made certain everyone had bought a ticket. As he moved up and down the aisle, he would call out: "Any more tickets! Any more tickets!"

Having finished selling tickets on the lower deck, he mounted the stairs to the upper deck and discovered the slippery, eggy mess on the floor. Stepping carefully over it, he called out loud and clear: "ANY MORE EGGS! ANY MORE EGGS!"

# JENNETTE LUKASIK

*Jennette Lukasik, a life-long Hamiltonian, attended McMaster University and Hamilton Teacher's college.*

*She is the author of many stories and memoirs, none of which have been published (until now). She has no distinguished awards to her credit. Nevertheless, she persists.*

## CONTEMPLATING TOES

I vigorously deny being a peeping-tom. I will, however, admit to peeking at strangers' toes.

Toes, my own and those of others, have always been of concern to me.

Exactly to what category of body parts do toes belong? Are they digits or appendages? When discussing them, it seems important to me to use the correct terminology. The *Gage Canadian Dictionary* describes toes as "one of the five end parts of the foot." I presume this definition hasn't changed since the 1983 printing of the dictionary.

Okay, I do admit that I hang onto things much longer than I should. My Grade 12 copy of Thomas Hardy's *Under the Greenwood Tree* does sit on a shelf next to the afore-mentioned dictionary. I don't even like the book, but I just may decide to reread it some summer afternoon, lacking other reading material.

The *Gage* dictionary of 1983 presents a valid description of toes, but does not fill my need for a classification. Further research leads me to understand that learned scholars, after much study of the subject, have grouped toes, along with fingers, in the category recognized as digits.

Such a grouping is woefully unfair to fingers. They belong in a category of their own. Fingers allow me to stroke the softness of a kitten, to hold the hand of a friend in the midst of sorrow. They allow me to create a personal work of art, no matter how amateurish. Fingers allow me to write whatever nonsensical thoughts come to my mind.

What value can we place on toes? The obvious is that toes are necessary for us to stand and walk. Toes allow a ballerina to take a stance that some of us can only admire or cringe at. Ingenious humans lacking fingers have skilfully adapted their toes to manage many functions carried out by others' fingers. These are all important uses not to be discounted, but certainly not at par with fingers.

The sad truth is that toes are rather odd objects. Fingers may be spoken of as slender, elegant, expressing movement and emotions, and a platform for displaying rings. Not so toes. From years of careful observation, I dare say that most of these ten digits at the ends of human feet verge on being somewhat ugly.

Personally, I have always considered my own toes to be the bane of my existence. Genetics decreed that my second toes on both feet position themselves as the alphas of the group by growing longer than the first toes. I consider this an act of rebellion, and insult to the proper order of things affecting my feet.

In taking on this position, these renegade toes have also earned the label "hammer toes." Far from representing me as Marvel Comic's latest female version of Thor—the woman who picked up Thor's hammer and took over his power, I am the bearer of odd digits. They are referred to as hammer toes, yet are powerless and are labelled as deformed. Don't even get me started on the issue of toe nails. I am presently searching Amazon and EBay in the hopes of finding a tiny hacksaw to cut nails grown thicker than a 2 x 4.

I have a female friend whose toes are perfect, truly perfect. The alpha toe is in charge, the other four face forward falling in perfect formation. The nail polish on her perfect toes is also perfect, never showing the slightest chip. It would be so easy to envy her until I am struck by the realization that her toes are like the Party members in Orwell's 1984. Lacking any personality of their own, strictly following the rules. No such adherents to report among my renegade toes, I am proud to proclaim.

As I carefully maneuver the streets of Hamilton, my eyes look for any crack, fissure, or uneven pavement that might cause me to do a face-plant on the city sidewalk. In summer, my downcast eyes are privy to a plethora of naked toes . . . toes, toes, everywhere I look. Toes in flip-flops and sandals, toes adorned with toe rings, nails polished, nails not polished, all confront me. Such an opportunity allows me to peek at strangers' toes. I'm able to form a basis of comparison to my own.

The other day, I noticed that the right baby toe of the young woman waiting to cross the street in front of me was in fact, only half a toe. What had happened? Had she been in an accident? With my curiosity piqued, I glanced at her other foot, careful not to stare as I never want to arouse suspicion. There may actually be a bylaw against toe peeking. I'd never want to be fined for such an infraction. How could I ever explain to family and friends? They'd think I was weird. As it turned out, the baby toe on her left foot was an exact match to the one on the right. She too was a victim of toe genetics.

When I encounter people with toes that are uglier than mine, I'm tempted to stop them and say, "I am so sorry about your toes." I refrain from doing that as it might just be that no one else gives any thought to toes.

# FINDING JOY IN UNEXPECTED PLACES

Tap! Sit! Observe!

"Move quickly," I remind myself. I tap my Presto card and lunge for the nearest available empty seat on the bus heading to downtown Hamilton. Previous experience and a sore, purple-hued hip courtesy of said bus have made me less choosy in my seat selection.

Closest unoccupied seat does just fine. Inevitably, this places me in the wheelchair area designated as *Priority Seating*. What the hell? At my age I have the right to declare myself to be a priority. Happy to be seated safely, I settle in for the twenty-minute ride to the MacNab Street Terminal.

"Are you okay?"

I turn in the direction of the question. A young woman occupies the seat beside me. Her forehead is furrowed, a look of concern on her pasty face. Brown eyes accented by stark black eyebrows are staring at me. I'm so startled by the perfectly painted eyebrows on the pale face, I don't answer immediately.

"Are you okay?" she repeats.

I sense that my loud sigh of relief at being seated safely before the bus heads out, hell bent for leather, may have been louder than I intended. It occurs to me the sound may have unnerved my seat mate. My children have often pointed out that it is an alarming sound. "Mom, stop doing that sigh. It scares us." Darn thing is, I've been doing it for so long I don't notice. It seems that others do.

"Thanks for asking. I'm fine. I'm just always so relieved to sit down before I fall." I answer with a loud chuckle, hoping to reassure her.

She looks back at me. I continue to stare at the painted eyebrows. "Very artistic," I think. I observe they are raised, rapidly moving up towards the furrows noticeably deepening on her forehead. Perhaps she's alarmed at the thought that I might be unable to remain upright and she'll be called upon to hoist me up off the dirty floor.

"It's a pretty nice day today, isn't it?" I continue talking, hoping to reassure her that I am sane and able to remain upright at the same time.

"No," she replies. "Yesterday was much nicer."

Inching my gaze down the row of seats, I shift my attention to the other passengers. Across from me sits a young woman, fuchsia streaks in her hair, holes in her jeans and brown Uggs on her feet. She catches my eye and smiles. I know she watched the scenario unfold. I welcome her smile as a sign that she may be the one person around me who doesn't think I'm bat-shit crazy.

Timmy's cups clutched in several passengers' hands announce the late winter ritual in the Kingdom of Tim Horton. This is not to be confused with the lesser realm of Pam's Coffee, which doesn't appear to have any rituals at the present time. It was declared many years ago that this rite in Timmy's Kingdom be designated "Roll up the Rim" and that it be celebrated far and wide. Adherents find great joy in purchasing a beverage in the hopes of winning one of many prizes offered. I silently wish them luck. To do so aloud might again undermine any appearance of sanity I'm trying to project.

My thoughts on coffee and by extension, donuts, are interrupted by the distinct sound of the wheelchair ramp being deployed. The bus driver approaches me. "I'm sorry ma'am but you'll have to move. There's a wheelchair incoming."

Ever mindful of moving quickly on the bus, I dart to the other side, again scoring a seat in the Priority Area. I breathe my sigh of relief and note that my inquisitor with the artful eyebrows has scurried to the back of the bus. The vacated seats are efficiently lifted leaving the area clear for the wheelchair.

"Hey, how are you ladies doing today? Nice to see you."

The driver sounds genuinely happy to welcome the wheelchair bound woman and her younger companion who is pushing her up the ramp.

"Hi Bob, great to see you again. Yeah, we're really good. Just setting off to see our social worker."

The driver heads back to his lofty seat at the wheel, leaving the young woman to secure the wheelchair in place. It's apparent that this ride and procedure happen often. The job is accomplished with great efficiency. The caregiver sits down, then jumps up. She extends her hand, "Mom, for a minute there, I thought you were going to stand up." Both women burst into laughter. "That wouldn't be so good," says the mother. "I'd be on the floor."

For the remainder of the trip I am privy to the pure joy and love so palpable between mother and daughter. Conversations between the two are enriched with smiles and giggles. Occasionally, the daughter opens a book in her hand. She's able to sense when her mother needs some rest. I notice the library book is titled *Living in a Dysfunctional Family.* The idea crosses my mind that I am witnessing the exact opposite. I see a loving, functional relationship so evident between the two people in front of me.

"Hey, I hear you're going to see the social." Young guy, hair shaved down to his scalp, full growth of beard on his face taps the daughter on her shoulder.

She nods a silent yes and smiles at him. "Me too," he announces. Anecdotes and information are exchanged about dealing with social workers. A bond is quickly established.

"You wanna hear something funny about a social worker?" The young woman smiles at her new friend.

"Sure," he says. He's open to hearing anything that might help him.

"Well, this social worker I knew, she's moved away now. She must make a hundred thousand dollars a year, maybe even more. I don't know, for sure. I think they make a lot. She told me she was a shoplifter." The woman pauses, waiting for a reaction.

"No way!"

"Yeah, she told me herself. Said she couldn't help it. Said she enjoyed the thrill of getting away with it." The daughter shrugs her shoulders.

"I gotta tell you I know what she means. I've shoplifted. There's nothing better than the feeling of getting away with it. Never been caught. I only do it in big stores. Don't wanna hurt some guy with a small business. Just wouldn't be right." The self-confessed thief smiles, content in feeling that he does the right thing.

The ride ends with arrival at the MacNab Street Terminal. Young bald guy and occasional shoplifter offers to accompany his new friend and confidant and her mother to the social. The pair smile and nod their agreement. Shoulders back, head held high the young man takes charge of the wheelchair. With confidence in every step he leads his newfound companions to their mutual destination.

Bienvenue! Willkommen! Welcome! Climb aboard!

Tap your Presto card! Sit back and observe!

# Afternoon on the Patio

Blue sky.

White clouds blend to pale grey at the edges.

Harvested garlic, dry garden soil brushed off the heads, lies on a table.

Six stalks to a bunch are tied together, hung to dry.

Freshly laundered shirts on the clothesline dance to the rhythm of the breeze.

Countries of origin: Vietnam, India, Peru, Haiti.

The workers in the factories, were they women, barricaded in, no escape route?

Did the Indian women wear saris to their factory jobs?

Did the Peruvian women wear brightly embroidered skirts and traditional *monteras* on their heads as their hands stitched the shirts drying on my clothes line?

I know nothing of their lives.

The Rose of Sharon is in full bloom, white flowers, dabs of magenta at the centres.

Above the blossoming shrub a wasp, enticed by the sweet odour of apple juice, is caught in a hanging bee-hive like trap.

Once in, there is no escape.

Frantically hitting against the glass sides it flies around.

Tired out, it gives up and drowns in the inviting treacherous juice.

I sense a metaphor for life and the choices we make.

Don't ponder! Enjoy the day!

Watch the red and white flag attached to the garden shed flap in the breeze.

Observe the multi-coloured, wind "thing-a-ma-jig" twirl around, creating a rainbow effect as it spins.

Look, as the mid-afternoon sun sparkles on the pool water, ripples of water catch the light, creating diamonds so bright I am forced to avert my eyes.

Shades pulled down on the patio provide shelter from the unyielding sun.

Shades stirred by a breeze clack against the metal supports of the patio roof.

Sunlight seeks and finds spaces in the drawn shades.

A shadowy pattern is cast onto patio stones.

Horizontal lines of light cross my writing paper.

The quiet of the neighbourhood is undisturbed by human voices.

Crows settle high in the branches of a dead tree in an adjoining yard.

They caw their anger into the air.

Leaves on the maple tree stir lazily in the soft blowing wind.

A whisper-like sound announces their existence.

Bees not tempted by apple juice hover over every orange and yellow flower in the garden circle.

Purpose is evident in each slow, deliberate movement.

A small, white butterfly flits erratically through the same garden and leaves.

I remain content to observe and enjoy all that surrounds me.

# MAUREEN MCMORROW

*Maureen McMorrow is a voracious reader and likes to pen her own observations of life. She enjoys the camaraderie and support of the Voice of Older Adults group.*

## THE VISITOR

She walked briskly up the tenement stairs. It was the grungy part of Gastown, a far cry from Vancouver the charming. The hallway stank of urine and cigarette butts. A greasy bulb cast a pathetic pool of light on the stained walls. Holding her cape close and her bag tightly, she reached the door. She knocked. No answer but loud groaning, and then nothing. "Jeannette, can you hear me? Jeannette, talk to me!"

The door refused to budge. The woman stepped back, raised her boot. The rotten wood was no match for a six-foot woman with sturdy Doc Martens. The door jamb crumbled. The light was dim. An old shower curtain shut out most of the day. A naked bulb struggled to life when the visitor pressed the dirty switch by the door. On a card table, mouldy bread had taken up permanent residence.

A head hung over the side of bare and rusted springs. Long and stringy hair covered the face of an emaciated woman. The visitor rushed to her side, turned her over and looked into her eyes. They were glazed and unseeing. "Damn it, Jeannette, you've done it again. That insulin needle isn't optional like all the other needles in this neighborhood!"

It wasn't really that much of a shock to this visitor. As a community nurse she had seen far worse on her rounds, kicking in more doors than she cared to think about.

Alcohol poisoning, all in a day's work. Sammy had wanted to die, he felt so bad. Not too bad to go back on the cheap red the next day. Hair of the dog, he always said.

The worst was finding young Jim hanging by the neck, his rosary half out of his shirt pocket. His last line of coke all used up, a sort of tidying up for the last hurrah. The inside of a cigarette pack bore his last will and testament. "Nurse, tell Mom I really did love her . . . ."

Then there was Milly, or "Milly the Meth Girl" as she was known in the hood. When she was straight, she would feed her two little daughters. Sometimes they even had a wash. The nurse hadn't come to see Milly, didn't even know her. But the door was open. Milly was on the floor. The little ones played with a mangy cat and paid no mind to their mother or the nurse. They had scratched their heads until they bled.

She couldn't think about any of that now. Jeannette was reacting to the insulin needle, coming out of the diabetic coma. "Welcome back, Jeannette. You nearly did it this time. What happened?"

Jeannette stared at her, weak but defiant. "I forgot. I was busy. It was bottle day. I got to have those bottles to get my smokes. You know that, Sheila."

"Well, at least you recognize me, that's a plus." The nurse took off her cape, hanging it high on the single hook. The cockroaches weren't likely to travel upwards. Even they seemed exhausted. Next step, the clean-up. Sheila took a face-cloth from her bag, dampened it in the slow trickle from the rusty tap in the corner. Almost tenderly, she wiped the grime from Jeannette's face. Jeannette closed her eyes and sighed. "What can I do?"

As she brushed the tangled hair, the nurse called Sheila replied as gently as possible. "Well, you can see your social worker and find somewhere decent to live. You have to look after yourself. You know what can happen. You could go blind. Your foot could get infected and be amputated."

Jeannette sighed again and made her usual promise. "Ya, okay, I'll do it tomorrow."

The nurse nodded, patted her hand. She took down her cape, shook off the solitary insect.

"So long, kiddo, see you soon." Only too soon, she thought.

# JUDY MENDELSON

*Judy Mendelson is a retired teacher of thirty-two years. She has two wonderful children, Joshua and Rachelle. She resides in Hamilton, Ontario, with Irwin Rodin, her husband of thirty years. New to The Voice of Older Adults group at the Hamilton Public Library, she discovered her voice. Judy has published two articles in* The Hamilton Jewish News. *She continues creating and learning the craft of writing.*

## CLIMBING DUNDURN STAIRS

D o you want to climb the Dundurn stairs?" My husband yelled from the kitchen.

Upstairs in my bedroom, I snuggled deeper into my warm comfy bed with my favourite comforter. I started creating excuses in my head why I didn't want to climb 329 steps in -7 degree weather early Sunday morning.

I have a headache

I'm too tired.

My knees are killing me.

I exercised three days ago.

It's kinda too late, I'm hungry.

I need time to file my taxes.

"Okay, sure," I answered, barely recognizing my own voice. "I'll be down in ten minutes."

On the way to the stairs, I didn't feel much better. Thinking about climbing the stairs made me tired. I started to think of more excuses, this time a little more creative, such as the steps might be closed down due to a huge snow storm on the way.

When we got to the edge of the stairs, I decided to go first. I didn't want my husband to somehow hear the thoughts in my head. Married couples tend to read each other's minds and we were no exception. When we got to the stairs, the air was crisp and there wasn't a cloud in the sky. Snow lay on the ground and I wondered where the squirrels were hiding. The last time we climbed the stairs, they were scampering around looking for nuts. They're probably sleeping in a warm comfy nest, I thought with some resignation.

By the time we got halfway up the stairs, I started to feel better. I smiled at a fellow climber and he smiled back and then he commented that it was a lot easier going down than climbing up. We laughed and felt the urge to pick up our pace to get to the top quicker so we could descend faster.

By the second time we made it to the top, my headache was gone. My knees didn't hurt and I wasn't tired at all. In fact, I had this surge of energy that made me want to hug the earth. Instead, I settled for hugging my husband.

The natural beauty of the area took my breath away. Tall trees with snow covering the tops of the branches reminded me of Merino homemade sweaters. Spring was trying to burst through the door but the cold air stood as a gatekeeper not allowing spring inside quite yet.

Halfway down the stairs, I noticed a vaguely familiar face running up the stairs in runner's gear, intent on getting to the top. In a split second I searched for recognition but instead I found my voice speaking.

"Hey, I know you," I exclaimed excitedly. "You're Stephen's mother. Do you remember me?"

She stopped running and said, "Yes, I know you. I saw you earlier on the steps."

"So, how are you?" She was my favourite volunteer twenty-four years ago when I taught kindergarten at Earl Kitchener Public School in Hamilton. Her son Stephen was one of my kindred spirits. He was a shy boy with white-blond hair and big, blue eyes. He loved to sit next to me at the round table and draw beautiful pictures. I remember worrying that maybe I should try to engage him to play with the toy cars or with the other boys at the block center. But instead Stephen liked to sit quietly and talk about his adventures with his younger brother, Michael. His mom volunteered in my class during holiday parties like Christmas and St. Valentine's Day.

"So how is Stephen? What's he doing now?" I inquired

"Stephen died, Ms. Mendelson. He had 4th stage bowel cancer. After the diagnosis he lived for a little while but he was in so much pain."

Her eyes watered but her voice was strong.

"We really miss him."

Smack! Life just threw me a hard ball and of course I missed it. My whole body went numb and I just wanted to evaporate like the Wicked Witch of the East in the *Wizard of Oz*.

"I am so, so sorry. I didn't know," I stammered.

"He fought so hard. Some of his art pieces are in the Art Gallery of Hamilton. His brother, Michael, graduated . . . ."

I think I went into shock because I don't remember what she told me about Michael.

Stephen was the only student I accepted an invitation from to his 5th birthday party in my entire teaching career. I remember struggling to make a decision as to whether it was appropriate for a teacher to attend one of her pupil's birthday parties. In the end, I was glad I had gone. Most of my students attended and I got to see them in a different light. At the party, we were content to just have fun with one another.

"I am so, so sorry," I repeated. "I didn't know. Are you still living in the little cottage downtown?"

"No," she answered. "We moved when Stephen was in seventh grade just around the corner from here."

At that point there was nothing more to say. We said our goodbyes and she raced up the stairs. I was in a daze but had to make a decision to either continue up the stairs which felt like a huge struggle or run down the stairs which I felt more inclined to do. I wanted to go back down the stairs, get into my car, drive home, take off my clothes and go back to bed.

Instead we plodded up the stairs one step at a time until we reached the top. We came back down and my husband asked if I wanted to do another one.

"No!" my mind screamed, "I don't want to." But I found myself climbing the stairs again. After all, Stephen's mother climbs the stairs. What a courageous women.

Tomorrow I will climb the stairs again. Maybe I will see Stephen's mother and I can offer her some support. I know one thing I'll do is block off the excuses that pop up in my mind. Instead of wasting time and making excuses, I will take hold of the day and, one step at a time, climb the Dundurn stairs until I reach the top.

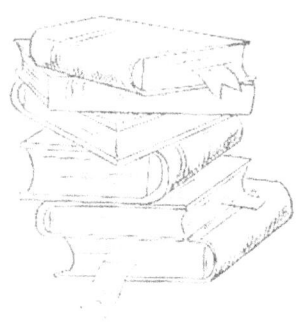

## Donald Trump Goes to Kindergarten

Yes, Donald, it's time for Show and Tell.

"No, Donald, you can't go first this week because you went first last week. Don't you remember?

"It's Enrique's turn to go first, then Justin and then you. It doesn't matter if Enrique's parents are from Mexico. Everyone is from a different country if you go back far enough except for the First Nations.

"No, Donald, Enrique's face is not dirty. People come in all shapes, colours and sizes. Enrique's has a lovely light brown colour.

"Enrique, you have a beautiful face with large, dark eyes and a cheery smile.

"Of course I like your face colour, too, Donald.

"Okay everybody, let's make a circle. We won't have enough time before the bell rings if we don't get started.

"Yes, Jessica?

"Donald won't keep his hands off you? He kissed you?

"Donald, what's our rule about touching and kissing other people at school?

"Yes, that's right, Donald. We don't touch anybody unless they want us to and we save kissing for the people in our families especially our moms and dads.

"Donald, move a little bit away from Jessica. In fact, why don't you sit next to Vladimir? No wait that's not such a great idea. You two are always getting into trouble when you play together. I know, why you don't sit next to Justin.

"Why don't you want to, Donald? Why? You and Justin have been friends for a long time.

"Justin took a car away from you at free play?

"Is that true, Justin? Did you take a car away from Donald?

"Saying sorry to Donald is the right thing to do, Justin. You are very thoughtful.

"Pardon me, Enrique? Donald took all of the toy cars and trucks away during free play and Justin was just trying to get one for you and one for him? Donald wasn't sharing?

"Is that true, Donald?

"Pardon me, Enrique?

"Donald built a big wall around all the toy cars and says that you can't have any of the toy cars? He wants you to put away all of the blocks?

"Donald, I know you want all of the toy cars and trucks for yourself but sometimes we have to let other people have a turn. Isn't it more important to have friends than to have all the toys for yourself? Justin and Enrique want to be your friend. And, Donald, you know our rule at school is if you build with the blocks, you need to put them away.

"Oh Donald, what do you mean you're firing me? Students can't fire their teachers."

# Donald Trump Goes to Kindergarten

Briiiiiiiiiiiiiiiiiiiiiiiiiiiiiiiiiiiiiiiiiiiiiiiiiiiiiiiiiiiiiiiii
iiiiiiiiiiiiiiiiiiiiiiiiiiiiiiiiiiiiiiiiiiiiiiiiiiiiiiiiiiiiiiiiiiiiiiiiiiiii-
iiiiiiiiiiiiiiiiiiiiiiiiing!

"Oh dear, girls and boys I just heard the recess bell. We can continue Show and Tell after recess.

"Donald, why are you crying and stamping your feet? I know we didn't get to you but we will after recess.

"What? What's wrong now?

"Who said you're a loser? Theresa called you a loser?

"Is that true, Theresa? Did you call Donald a loser?

"You need to apologize. There are no losers in this classroom. Everyone is a winner.

"Come here, Donald, let me give you a hug to cheer you up.

"Donald, when you grow up, you can be anything you put your mind to it. You can even grow up and be the president of the United States of America.

"Are you feeling better now, Donald?

"Great ,now let go. Donald, let go. Donald, you're squeezing me a bit too hard. Donald. Donald!!!!"

# SIMONE ROTSTEIN

*Simone Rotstein has been writing for about six years. She enjoys the process and the support of her writing group.*

## LEEKY MEATBALLS

I enjoy preparing food and cook almost every day. Over the years, the food I make has transformed from regular North American fare to the Middle Eastern cuisine on which I grew up. I remember my mother spending hours in the kitchen preparing time and labour intensive dishes; vegetables that were stuffed into grape leaves, tomatoes or peppers; chicken and fish cooked in an aromatic stew and served over couscous; small savoury pastries shaped into triangle or cigar shapes using filo dough; and dried prunes or dates stuffed with nuts and then simmered in a sugary syrup. These smells, tastes and visuals evoke another life.

When my children were small and I was working, expediency was very important. Meals needed to be on the table within a short time to avoid meltdowns and crabby kids. I rotated several easy meals over a week and we ate, not inspired, but healthy and well. The idea of recreating time-consuming recipes was rarely in my sight. Very occasionally, for a special meal, I would make a dish conjuring up my past.

It was my daughter who began to ask me to prepare things from my heritage. "It's my heritage too," she said. "I need to learn how to make a good shakshuka." And so, I started. I would change an ordinary chicken dish to one with Middle Eastern flavours. I roasted eggplants and prepared okra and suddenly I was satisfying a need I didn't know I craved.

Once a year, I prepare what my children called *leeky meatballs*. I wash, chop and cook the leeks before combining them with ground meat and spices and forming small patties. The sauce, seasoned with garlic and lots of lemon juice, simmers on the stove, all set to receive the patties. The scent wafts through our home as the patties cook, arousing memories. It brings me back to a small kitchen in Egypt, where the cook, Ibrahim, chopped and sautéed vegetables in preparation of our lunch. It reminds me of de Vimy Street, in Montreal, and my mother endeavouring to recreate our familiar foods with limited ingredients.

The aroma speaks of Alexandria, my mother and my daughter's words, "Mom, we need to preserve our heritage." As I serve the dish, I feel content. The *leeky meatballs* straddle my worlds, and memories linger in my life.

## CEREBRAL PALSY DIAGNOSIS

With the birth of our daughter, Ed and I were in heaven. After many disappointments, we had a wonderful baby who looked perfect, smelled delicious and filled us with joy. We marvelled at everything she did; her cooing, her smiling and her kicking. We named her Alysa after Ed's father and because, in Hebrew, it means joy. We watched her every achievement with pride and gratitude; she was a pleasure.

At eight months, Alysa was still unable to sit without support and we knew something was seriously wrong. It had been a difficult birth but her Apgar score, assessed shortly after the birth, had been very good, indicating she was a well-baby. She was an alert and lively child and she couldn't sit up by herself. We trudged to our doctor for another visit, hoping for some reassuring words. We left with our young daughter and a referral to a paediatric-neurologist.

Dr. Neil Morris was a large bear of a man, sporting an equally large, unkempt beard and piercing eyes. His office was a functional, though dreary, place with worn furniture. This was a place of work and the state of the physical environment had little role. He listened to us, never interrupting, carefully watching Alysa and ourselves. We explained what we had noticed, Alysa's birth experience, and, oh yes, that bloody tap caused by the amniocentesis.

I was offered an amniocentesis, to check for aberrations in the fetus, since I had endured three miscarriages with abnormalities observed on two of them. The third I had miscarried during a break at work. I had gone to the washroom and while sitting on the toilet lost the fetus. In a panic, I flushed it. It seemed the only option at the time.

Now, we sat at another medical clinic hoping for some answers and reassurances. After we finished giving our observations, the physician picked up Alysa and examined her, holding her gently and manipulating her neck, her arms and her legs. The room was still, except for Alysa, acting as if this was an innovative playtime, squealing and smiling broadly. There was something reassuring about having this bear of a man tending my daughter.

Finally, turning to us, he said, "First, I want to tell you you will have more *naches* then sorrow from your daughter." *Naches* is a Yiddish term used to describe pride and gratification and especially pride and gratification at the achievements of one's children. Ed and I looked at each other and both of us visibly relaxed.

He went on to tell us that Alysa had cerebral palsy. It is a condition marked by impaired muscle coordination. In Alysa's case, her right side was affected. Both her right arm and her right leg were weak and unlikely to recover from a trauma to her brain. Cerebral palsy affects body movement, muscle control, tone and reflex, and a person's coordination, posture and balance. Hence she was unable to sit up on her own at eight months. There is no cure for cerebral palsy, only therapy and adaptations to help alleviate the symptoms. We were referred to Chedoke Hospital, which, at the time, tended to children with disabilities. It catered to children who needed support in order to realize their potential. And so began a life filled with physiotherapists, occupational therapists, social workers, orthopaedic surgeons, ophthalmologists and paediatricians.

While Alysa's intellectual and verbal development proceeded normally, her physical skills, particularly her mobility, were much delayed. At about a year, she began to move by bumming across the floor. She used her left hand to navigate to different places. Even outdoors she moved on her behind. We chopped down the mulberry tree in our backyard as all her clothes became permanently stained purple. She was almost two before she stood on her legs and walked, pushing a wooden wagon for support. It was comparable to older people using a walker. By that time, we had our second child, our son, Joshua.

Over the next two years, Alysa, with the help of a brace on her right leg, became more and more proficient at walking around. Her language was very well-developed and she was an inquisitive child. She was barely two and a half when she informed us that she needed to go to school and so she began, at Montessori.

It always amazed me that a child who needed so much assistance was so determined and independent.

Alysa must have been almost four years old when we decided it was time she learned how to walk up the stairs, using the railing for support. I crouched at her feet, lifting one foot after the other and placing it on the next step, following the instructions of the physiotherapist. We spent almost an hour navigating the bottom three steps, up and down, up and down. My son, just over eighteen months old, had been playing close to us, walking back and forth, while watching his older sister's progress. Without any warning, he climbed past us and walked straight up the whole flight of stairs. At the top, he looked down at us, a huge grin on his face.

My frustration flared. I thought, "How unfair life is!" Yet, marvelled at the ease my son had with his mobility and at the lack of jealousy Alysa exhibited. My daughter and I continued practicing on the bottom three steps.

## PILGRIMAGE

Gerard, the owner of El Sol Verde Lodge in Costa Rica, serves Ed and I breakfast as he explains how to get to the Rincón de la Vieja Volcano. "You just follow the road. It will twist and turn and you'll drive about forty-five minutes. Once you get there, get your tickets and then follow the signs leading up to the Hidden Falls."

"Where can I buy a bouquet of flowers?" I ask him.

"Why would you buy flowers? There are plenty here." He gestures to the beautiful gardens of the Lodge. "Alysa liked those particularly," pointing to the bougainvillea as he passes me some shears.

He gives us the lunch box his wife, Ingrid, has packed for us, lays a hand on us and wishes us well. After several days travelling in Costa Rica, we know more than enough about twisty, pot-holed roads and we are soon at the foot of the mountain.

"What beautiful flowers. Are they for me?" jokes the ticket vendor.

I hesitate and then reply, "For my daughter."

His eyes pierce into me and then, with both hands, he touches his heart.

The sun beats down as we begin our climb. We hike over rocks, using our hands to secure ourselves. We ford streams, hopping from stone to stone to keep our feet dry. We balance on rope bridges as they sway under our weight. We trudge across sun-drenched meadows cloaked in yellow and red flowers. The trek is arduous, long and beautiful. And I wonder, "How did my daughter navigate this hike with her disability?"

We hear the roar before we see it.

"We're close now," Ed says.

A feeling of tightness spreads through my body as I clutch the bouquet of flowers. Ed leads the way down a short, rocky trail, which turns sharply around a corner. The wind picks up, thrashing at us. My feet stumble on the damp, slick stones and I lurch around trying to stabilize myself.

"Be careful!" Ed yells, his terrified voice straining to be heard over the roar of the rushing water. Exhausted after our three hour ascent, we cling to each other, staring at the waterfall and the surrounding area; the clear blue sky, the rich, verdant vegetation and the neighbouring mountain tops and valleys.

Ed loses his footing and I shout, grabbing at his hand. We retreat, then slowly inch closer to the falls, skirting the water, and gape down, twenty-five meters straight down the cascading waters. We back away, overcome. Again, we move closer to the gurgling stream. It meanders to the edge of the mountain before flowing down the mountainside. Sorrow engulfs me as I envisage my daughter tumbling down the side of the mountain. I choose one flower; throw it into the stream and watch as it rushes over the side and cartwheels down the mountainside. Then, another flower and another until there are none left. We stand together in silence. Ed chants a prayer. We are subdued as we turn around to make our way back up the trail to an open field and into the relentless wind. We find shelter behind an outcrop and I cry at the injustice of it all.

Stillness slowly descends on us. Ed says, "I'm going back to the waterfalls."

I am terrified. "You're going to fall! Then what will I do? I can't lose you as well as Alysa."

He is determined and I follow. We make our way down the trail, inching over the stones and gaze at the backdrop. Large, graceful birds circle through the vast sky, catching thermal winds, soaring high in the atmosphere before gradually gliding downward. A few white, fluffy clouds drift through the azure blue background. The hills rise around us, majestic and luxuriant. The only sounds are our breathing, and the bubbling, churning water. The area around the falls is now more familiar and safer.

"This must be where they sat and had their lunch," I say, pointing to some flat rocks at the side of the falls.

"Looks like it," Ed answers. "Then they would have crossed the stream to get to Hidden Falls."

We both stare at the stream.

"We're not crossing the stream!" I insist.

Lauren and Stephanie crossed the stream and went ahead to Hidden Falls. Shauna and Alysa lingered after eating their lunch and then stood up to join their friends at the next set of falls. Alysa never made it.

We visualize the flowers, stranded in a pool on a ledge far below, and imagine our daughter. It is implausible, yet, so very real. We are able to situate Alysa here. We envision her walking, talking and laughing. This journey is a pilgrimage to reclaim our daughter. The loss is no less. The pain does not abate. We quietly turn around and head back, up the trail away from the falls. We once more find refuge at our outcrop.

We stood right at the place where Alysa fell. It was an accident. One slip of the foot and down . . . The climb up to the falls was gruelling. I kept on thinking, "I need two hands. How did she do it?" Her tenacity and determination overcame her disability and sustained her. My admiration for Alysa is huge. Her spirit grows in me. She is with me.'

At the river, where Alysa fell, it is wildly beautiful. She so much enjoyed life and had many experiences in her short life. At the falls, where she slipped down, we said goodbye. She is in a beautiful place and at peace.

We complete our journey down the mountain.

# JEAN RYAN

*Jean Ryan has had stories published in two anthologies:* In the Wings: Stories of Forgotten Women *and in* Engraved: Canadian Stories of World War One.

## LIP SMACKING

P ale, bloodless post-menopausal lips . . . ," Dolores no longer remembered where she first came upon the description, only that it caused her then pre-menopausal self to shudder. The words had evoked an immediate visual on the ever changing 3-D projection in her mind. The mouths of all her aunts and her grandmother skipped along the screen, some smiling, others pursed, and a few merely at rest.

Whenever it had happened, it was the start of a long habit, a hobby if you will, of looking at women's lips, that led to focusing on the broader area of the mouth. Riding the TTC subway or the GO commuter train, she would glance through a screen of lashes to scan the occupants of the seats opposite.

*That one had a full lower lip—somewhat pouty. There's a perfect cupid's bow. Over there is a poorly defined mouth, edges bleeding out onto the general facial landscape. She ought to try a lip liner; it would provide definition and a younger appearance.*

Over the years, her internal commentary became more acerbic and judgmental. At some point, she began determining character traits and personality from the contours of the mouths.

*That one's a piece of work. Just look at that mouth, all hard lines. I bet she grinds her teeth too! Oh, and over there, smoker, I'm sure she was a smoker. Her lips look like they were pulled together by a drawstring. And, there, right there! She must have really bad false teeth. Poor thing, I wonder if she's on welfare, no, what do they call it now, social assistance. If not that, then what's her problem? 'cause those lips are stretched over those falsies. Falsies? Weren't they what we called padded thingies? You tucked them into you bra to look like you had bigger bazooms. Where was I? Oh yeah, those pathetic lips. If she got a bigger set of dentures, she'd start looking like a Ubangi. I remember those photos from* National Geographic.

Dolores' head snapped up with a start.

*Where am I? Oh dear, I missed my stop. I have to get off the subway and go back the other way. I might miss my dentist's appointment. That reminds me, that hygienist needs to change her lipstick, she has nice firm young lips, but the colour she wears is all wrong. She should try a nice pale pink, more suitable for a*

*woman her age. Dark red is too harsh, she looks like a hooker. Do*
*they say "hooker" anymore?*

As Dolores steadied herself on her three-footed cane, she
didn't notice the heads that swiveled in her direction as she
left. Two forty-something ladies sitting near the doors turned
to each other with open-mouthed wonder.

"Did you see that?"

"I did, but I couldn't believe it."

"If I ever start looking like that, just shoot me."

"I'm thinking I'll be in the next room at the home and may
not have it together enough to tell you. Well really, how do
you think she arrived at that particular look?"

"Hmmm . . . okay, so here's my guess. You apply heavy
cover-up type foundation all around the lips. Then get a candy
apple red lip liner and draw a large lip outline. Then use an
even brighter, more intense red and fill in. Blot and reapply a
few times and voila! The perfect totally weird lips! Eat your
heart out Mick Jagger

# BRENDA WHITEFORD

*I'm Brenda Whiteford, also known as karaoke singer "BB." I'm originally from Ingersoll, Ontario, but have lived in Hamilton since I was fifteen, and I am now sixty-two. I started writing children's stories after my husband passed away. The public library and writing circle have brought me much satisfaction and helped my writing.*

## WHEN I WAS FIVE I WANTED TO BE ...

When I was five, more than anything, I wanted to be . . . mmmmmm . . .

One Sunday morning I walked up to the minister and impatiently waited for my turn to talk to him.

"Excuse me, Mr. Minister, but I have a question for you."

"Yes, little one, what is it?"

"Well, I want to be God. Can I?"

"You mean in the Sunday School play?"

"No," I said. "I just really want to be God."

"Well." He laughed and I got mad and cried and he said, "Well, you can't be God."

"Why can't I be God?" I asked.

"Well, no one can be God!" he explained.

I felt broken hearted.

"You're a little angel," he said. "Now run along."

After that I was in a Sunday School play and I played an angel. I learned so many lines and quotes from the Bible. It was amazing!

Everyone said I made a good angel.

After church, my friend Christina and I played in my backyard.

My father grew grapes, so we were eating them, and Christina said, "Old Mrs. Young's grapes taste better." She said that old Mrs. Young had given her mother a handful of grapes and they tasted better.

We got to thinking it over and decided we'd just go to Old Mrs. Young's backyard and have a few. She shouldn't mind, we thought. She has lots! The next thing we knew, we were in Old Mrs. Young's fenced-in backyard, eating her grapes.

All of a sudden, we heard the front door open and Old Mrs. Young step out onto her front porch. Then we could hear her step down her front steps. Next, we heard her walking towards her backyard. There was nowhere to go, so we opened her backdoor and hid in her house.

Christina hid in the fronthall closet and I hid in the bedroom closet.

When Old Mrs. Young came into her kitchen, Christina went out the frontdoor and ran all the way home, but I was still in her bedroom closet.

CRASH! Old Mrs. Young knocked something over. She took her time cleaning it up, and when she was done, she walked into her bedroom. She knelt beside her bed and started praying.

I did a little praying myself. "Oh please, God, don't let her find me!"

First she talked about her bad health and the bad health of others she knew. And I had to go to the bathroom.

Then, Old Mrs. Young really got sad. She started to talk about all her sins, and she had a long list of them. Why, she was crying and praying, praying and crying.

Oh, I felt sorry for her, so that was it, I jumped out of her closet and said: "Glory to God in the Highest; And Peace on earth; Good will towards men; For unto you is born this day; In the City of David; A Savior which is Christ the Lord; And you will find the babe; Wrapped in swaddling clothes; And lying in a manger."

Then I hollered: "GOD FORGIVES YOU! YOU ARE FORGIVEN, MRS. YOUNG!"

She saw the very best of my part in the Sunday School play with all the actions and everything.

Old Mrs. Young had no idea where I came from. She opened her eyes, then she said: "God, it's really you! And you've appeared before me in the form of an innocent child." Old Mrs. Young rejoiced. "I have been forgiven!" she said.

I didn't have the heart to tell her the truth and, well, I kind of liked the idea of being God. I really did! So, I just smiled and said, "Yes I'm God."

Old Mrs. Young was beside herself, laughing and crying, praying and kneeling down in front of me. "Oh, thank you, God! Oh, thank you!" she said, "for forgiving me of my sins." Then she said, "Can I get you anything?"

The first thing I thought of was toys, but I thought I'd better not ask for that. "Whatever you want to give me is fine," I said.

Old Mrs. Young was hopping around, laughing and singing. With that, we went into the kitchen. She asked, "Would you like some milk?" and before I could answer, she asked, "Would you like some cookies?"

I smiled.

I loved being God! She was happy. I was happy! Her eyes looked funny, but that was okay. Perhaps she was a little crazy, but that was okay. I loved being God.

When Old Mrs. Young went into the bathroom, I left and went home.

In the morning, I found her back door open, so walked right in saying, "It's okay, Mrs. Young. It's just God. I'm here!"

I loved being God, so I continued to go to Mrs. Young's house and say nice things out of the bible. Quotes I learned from Sunday school. Forgiveness knows no limits; love your neighbour as yourself; love the Lord your God with all your heart. It was all going oh so well, and then trouble happened.

Old Mrs. Young sipped her tea and as she looked across her kitchen table, she looked down at me and said, "I'm ill, God. I'm ill. Heal me, God! Heal me!"

"I'm sorry," I said quickly, but God has to go." Then I slid down off my chair, left her house, and ran all the way home. I didn't know it, but she followed me home.

Old Mrs. Young stood outside my house and stared. She said, "That's the Whiteford people's house," and then she went back home, feeling angry, feeling foolish!

That night, when I was upstairs in my bedroom all alone, fast asleep, Old Mrs. Young left her house, walked to my house, climbed up a big, old chestnut tree in front of our house, leapt onto my dad's roof, opened a little window, climbed down onto a chair, and walked over to my bed.

In the loudest voice she had, she yelled: "You're not God! You're Stan's daughter!"

I woke up. My mom and dad woke up. They stood at the bottom of the stairway very scared.

"What's going on?" gasped Dad as he turned on the light.

So I said, "Praise the Lord. You've been healed Mrs. Young!"

"Why are you in our house . . . ," my parents yelled, " . . . in little Brenda's room?"

Old Mrs. Young looked at me and ripples of wrinkles crossed her forehead as she looked around the room in a bewildered state of mind before going out the same way she had come in. Neighbours across the street said, "Is that Old Mrs. Young? Why is she climbing down Stan's tree?"

All the while, I sang, "Praise him; All the little children; God is love! God is love!"

As for me, I went back to bed happy.

Thank you, God, for letting me be God! I thought. It's exactly what I wanted to be, and God had answered my prayer. Isn't life great!

Meanwhile, my mom and dad were confused. "We will talk to little Brenda in the morning," they agreed as they both went back to bed.

When Old Mrs. Young arrived home, she sat alone in her kitchen, sipping her tea, and she thought about all the things little Brenda had said, and she wasn't angry anymore.

The next Sunday morning, the Sunday School teacher, Natasha, played the piano. A teenaged girl named Avery sang "How Great Thou Art." A manly boy named Darren narrated the play. Next, in full costume, four little angels: Yasmine, Zoé , Keira and Juliette leaped onto the stage.

Then, in walked Old Mrs. Young, just as the play was about to begin.

Oh, but in the loudest voices they had, the Whiteford girls, Donna, Betty, Eleanor and little Brenda yelled: "Welcome to church Mrs. Young!"

Then everyone laughed . . . including Old Mrs. Young.

# My Daddy's Gonna Worry

It was late September,
And the air was sweet,
Many, many, girls I'd like to meet,
But I got a job and I'm doing fine,
Since I bought that Ford of mine.

Chorus:
And I'm off . . . doo doo doo,
Down the road . . . La La La,
Burn'n gas . . . Ha Ha Ha,
My Daddy's gonna worry cause I move too fast.

My motorcycle is a mean machine,
I broke my leg—then I ditched that thing,
Now, I'm truckin' on down to my Daddy's farm,
I'll stick with that Ford,
It won't do me no wrong.

Now I'll stop for awhile at the bakery shop,
Buy all the sweets while they're hot,
It was there and then,
That I met my girl,
Verda you set my heart awhirl.

I played guitar at a famous doo,
Verda, you know, she played there too,
Won't see my Verda till another day,
I'll tip my hat and slip away.

Verda Lidster you're very sweet,
One of a kind you can't be beat,
Marry me and you won't go wrong,
Honey, I'll make your life a song.

The minister said God bless this day,
Kiss the bride and slip away,
Down to the falls in the summertime,
Longing to find a motel sign.

Mom's got the key and Dad opens the door,
Tribulations they are no more,
The answers I know cause I'm no fool,
Morning sunshine is shining through.

This family's growing up can't you see,
My kids, I think, they look like me,
Sometimes I wish I had a son,
The Whiteford name must carry on.

I'm glad you know it turned out alright,
Four pretty daughters and a lovely wife,
You know it doesnt matter if you walk or crawl,
As long as you feel like ten feet tall.

One thing for sure,
Life is so sweet,
A rhyme in your head,
A movement in your feet,
A hardy word said, a lasting smile,
Verda you make your life worthwhile.

*Dedicated to the memory of our parents, Stan and Verda Whiteford*

# KATHY WOLSEY

*Kathy Wolsey has found inspiration and encouragement from the older adult writing circle at the Hamilton Public Library. Writing has always been her passion. She is proud to be part of this anthology.*

## THE STORY OF MY GUIDE DOGS: SAD FAREWELL, NEW BEGINNING

### GRADUATION DAY

This will be my third graduation from the Canine Vision program at the Lions Foundation of Canada. My first boy was Percy and then next came Gibson. Now Oakley and I are graduating after weeks of intensive training. Graduation Day brings a bushel of emotions. It is met with excitement that the course is over and we will be heading home. Anticipation.

Who will attend the evening celebration: friends, family, your dog's foster family, sponsor or breeder if the dog was donated? Regret as we say goodbye to the people we have lived with for the past number of weeks. It is sad for the dogs leaving their quadruped and biped friends. Apprehension. It is one thing working with the dog guides in the controlled setting of the school. The trainers are always available. Your outside life has been put on hold. What will happen when we get home? It will be a different lifestyle for the new dog guide handlers. They have to adjust their lives to having a service dog at their side. The experienced dog guide handlers understand that the hard work now begins; the new dog has to learn the regular routine of his or her new home and life.

THE DAY OF GRADUATION IS busy. The official paperwork is completed. We sign a contract that we will be responsible for the health and well being of our dog guides. There is time to ask any additional questions or concerns of our trainers. We need to know what food variety our dogs have been eating: beef, chicken or lamb. We are given enough food to last for a few days to take home. We give our dogs a bath with the assistance of the trainer. A veterinarian may check them out for any other health concerns. We are to schedule a visit with our own vet within two weeks of arriving home.

At dinner, everyone sits together instead of sitting at separate tables with class mates. After each of us has our meal, the trainers join us. There is much conversation and laughter. Humorous incidents are recalled. We remember the early days of being with our dogs. The difference between what they were like then compared to the dogs lying quietly at our side is astonishing. We marvel at the development of our dogs and at our own abilities.

We don't want the dinner to end. When we leave the table we are no longer students but graduates.

Everyone returns to their rooms. The dining hall and lecture area are transformed into a reception area and auditorium. Dozens of folded chairs are set up for the guests. Each graduating class meets at a designated area. We proceed in together with our trainers. It can be hectic if there are several classes graduating on the same evening. The school has six programs: Canine Vision, Hearing, Service, Seizure Response, Autism Assistance and Diabetic Alert.

After the ceremony, we meet with our guests and the foster families, sponsors or breeders if they are present. It is very emotional. Tears of happiness are shed as we hear stories of our dog's puppy life. There are heart warming stories of why a dog may have been sponsored, in memory of a loved one or named after a former dog guide.

At the end of the night, the graduates try to locate their classmates and trainers in the crowds of people. For many, they will not see each other again. Hugs, tears and goodbyes are exchanged.

Kathy Wolsey

PERCY (OCTOBER 2004 – JANUARY 2005)

We graduated in October 2004. When we arrived home, we were greeted by Tessa, a Cocker Spaniel. She was my late husband's support dog. A year ago, she lost her job and constant companion when he passed away. Would Tessa and Percy get along? They bonded instantly. In the condo they were inseparable. She slept at one end of the couch and he lay at the other. A picture shows Percy looking around a corner, Tessa crouched under him staring in the same direction. I took them separately for walks. It gave Tessa and me some alone-time.

On our first day home, Percy and I went for a walk so he could get acquainted with the neighbourhood. He broke away from me. What did I do wrong? He did it again. The number of instances increased. If he saw another dog, cat, bird or anything moving, he went after it. It didn't matter if he was in or out of harness. When he was bad, he hung his head and looked guilty and remorseful. That was until the next time. I contacted the school. The trainer came out to help me. He assured me I was handling Percy properly. I kept in touch with them. It wasn't getting any better.

One night, he was about to run across a busy intersection. There was only one way to stop him. I slammed my body and arms around a hydro pole to keep hold of him. I was hurt, bruised and sore.

On a Saturday in January, I attended a neighbourhood meeting. He misbehaved on the way there.

When my friend saw us, she asked, "What did he do? He looks guilty."

"He tried to go after another dog," I said.

The snow storm that day started slowly. Soon it became a major downfall. The meeting ended early so people could get home. I declined offers of a ride. It was only four blocks to my condominium. The snow was blowing and drifting. We crossed the road to our street. Percy was about to bolt. "If you go, I can't stop you. And if you go, I don't know how I will get home." He stopped pulling. It was as though he understood the gravity of the situation.

On Monday morning I contacted the head trainer. "Percy still has problems," I said. I expected we would return to the school for more instructions. I was not prepared for his answer.

"Kathy, we know how hard you have worked with Percy. We're going to take him back." I started to cry. "You have done everything possible," he assured me. "We're concerned for your safety."

I packed up his bed, food dishes and toys. A trainer arrived in the afternoon. She said, "Let's sit down and talk. Tell me what's been going on."

I told her how he would break away from me, how he dragged me across the street and how he ran after anything that moved. He knocked me over several times. I was even nervous taking him for bathroom relief. "My white cane never ran me into poles or dragged me across the street," I cried.

"Kathy, you have not had a guide dog. I start a class at the end of February. There is a place for you, if you want it."

"I'm not sure." I hesitated.

"At any time, if you want to return home, with or without a dog, we will bring you home immediately."

That's how I ended up being in the last class of 2004 and the first class of 2005.

And Percy . . . he retired to a farm where he can chase all the animals he wants.

## GIBSON (FEBRUARY 24, 2005 - FEBRUARY 12, 2016)

Percy and Gibson were as different in temperament as they were in appearance. Percy had the huge head and broad chest of a Lab and was almost pure white. Gibson was jet black. He was long and lean. In harness, Gibson was all business.

We graduated on St. Patrick's Day, 2005. When we were at the school, there was no other world except the dogs. On our first day home, I took Gibson to Jackson Square, a shopping mall within walking distance. We toured the mall. I showed him where the bank was, the post office, the library. Our last stop was the Farmer's Market.

Instead of retracing our steps through the mall, we exited the market onto York Blvd. As we approached Copps Coliseum, the doors flew open and hundreds of excited children ran out. Since I had been in Oakville, I forgot it was March break. *Disney on Ice* is the attraction at the entertainment centre during the holidays. The children were racing and running eastward as their parents tried to keep up with them. Gibson and I were headed in the opposite direction. The mall doors were too far away for us to get back inside. I kept commanding Gibson, "Forward. Forward. Forward." It took ten minutes before we cleared the mob. That was his introduction to his new home town. Amazingly it was his home for the next ten years, eleven months and two weeks. He was born to be a guide dog. He conducted his duties right to the end. On February 12, 2016, we arrived home after a morning of errands. I took him out of harness. He went down, never to get back up.

OAKLEY (MAY 3, 2016 - PRESENT)

After the graduation dinner we went back to our room. My sister and stepson were attending the ceremony. Oakley and I would go home with them that night.

The suitcases sat open on the bed. Oakley is a very curious dog. He looks in any bag or box. It makes no difference if there is anything inside or not. He laid his chin on the bed and watched me put clothes, shoes, sweaters and a jacket into the suitcase.

"We're going home," I told him as I scratched his head. "You poor little fellow, you don't even know where home is."

Oakley, a yellow Labrador Retreiver, was born in Breslau, Ontario, at the kennels of the Lions Foundation. At eight weeks, he moved to his foster family in a suburb of Toronto, where he completed the first stage of his development as a "dog guide in training." He was just under a year old when he returned to the Lions Foundation. He began his official instruction with a trainer from Canine Vision Canada (CVC). Then it was time for him to be matched with a visually impaired/blind person. That match was with me. We were together their for two weeks. Our days were filled with different training exercises, working together and lots of walking. Then, he came home with me to my condominium in downtown Hamilton.

He went from his foster family, to a trainer and his buddies in the kennels and finally to me. What a lot of changes for an eighteen-month-old puppy.

### TWO YEARS LATER: MAY 2018

Oakley has matured to be a competent and trustworthy guide dog. Now, when I say, "Take us home," he knows where to go. We walk in harmony; if I am slower that day, he slows his pace. If I'm in a hurry, he quickens his steps to match mine.

He is alert to dangerous situations. Once, as we walked to the shopping mall, he stopped and would not move. Not even when I commanded, "Forward." I realized something was wrong. So I said, "Find the way." He was up and guided us around a closed and fenced off sidewalk.

Out of harness, he is a puppy at heart. And yes, he still is curious and has to look in every bag or box, even if it is empty. He chases his tail in one direction, whirls around and chases it the opposite way. He still wants lots of loving and does not hesitate to sit on my lap, all seventy pounds of him.

He is only three and a half years old. There are many years ahead for us to explore and have adventures.

# Faithful Friend

Four legs and a wagging tail
    A wet nose and keen ears
        He shows more sense
            than many with two
My faithful friend

Long talks we do have, confidences shared
    always ready to listen
        No judgment, no disapproval,
           Only forgiveness
              and understanding
My faithful friend

Together we have walked,
      We have trekked,
            We have travelled
                  Streets, buses, trains
My faithful friend


Never apart are we
      He watches my every step,
           My every move
                Ever diligent, always protective
My faithful friend
My guide dog
      My Gibson

At eight weeks, Gibson left home
    Began life at Lions Foundation of Canada
        Gibson in Canine Vision
            to see for those who can't
                Does he have what it takes?
My faithful friend


Foster care came first,
    Puppy in green coat
        Future guide dog it does say
            Rules and lessons to learn
Traffic, schools, crowds, stores
    Does he panic?
        Does he get confused?
My faithful friend

Pass he does, now to work
    Green coat gone, harness on
        He likes to work and please
            Traffic, schools, crowds, stores
                Obstacles everywhere
My faithful friend


Harness handle up,
    he must learn how
        Can he find the safest route?
            Can he guide safely through?
My faithful friend

Many months, constant work,
    Treats and praise
        How well he does
            and soon, prepare,
                to get ready, to meet . . .
My faithful friend

Excitement, people arrive,
    Many hands lift his harness
        Some are firm, some nervous,
            One, two, three days and then . . .
                Who will be *his* one?
My faithful friend

Anxious I wait,
     Which dog will it be?
          Black, brown or white
There is the knock
I open the door,
     There he is . . .
          It's Gibson,
               Gorgeous Gibson of Rabdalor


More than ten years have passed
     Gibson and I have lived much in those years
          Birth, life and death we have shared
               Always at my side, together we go
My faithful friend,
     My guide dog,
          My Gibson

***Gorgeous Gibson of Rabalor***
(Gibbs, Gibbey, Mr. Gibbs)
June 30, 2003 – Feb. 12, 2016


Worked as a Guide Dog: Feb. 26, 2005 - Feb. 12, 2016

Sketch created by Carolyn Lehmann, a dear friend

# VIRGINIA ASHBERRY

## Afterword

Right from the beginning . . . from the very first time I met with this group, I knew that this was what I had been missing since moving to Hamilton. "The Voice of Older Adults" group is a truly varied cross section of the older community, every single one actively engaged in the act of self-discovery through writing about their past and present, fantasy and future, poetry and . . . even limericks!

Writing is just about the best thing you can do to keep yourself in touch with feelings about yourself and others in a meaningful way. It is a true commitment, this act of writing a story. There is something deeper, more resilient and lasting when you commit to a beginning, middle and an end. Not just the utilitarian act of tapping out an email or text. This is something you thought hard about before you put it on paper, and before you dared to share it with the group. It is your truth, as you know, remember and feel it.

This book, *The Voice of Older Adults,* is filled with seventeen important lives and their events. More important because they have put it on paper, and therefore, will endure.

I could press the back of my hand to my forehead and pretend that the act of assembling these stories from seventeen writers has been tortuous . . . but it has not. Modern technology is amazing at reducing the effort, and working with so many understanding and mature writers has been a joy.

## Acknowledgements

All of the authors in *The Voice of Older Adults* wish to thank Laurie Kallis for her outstanding work as the graphic designer and typesetter for this anthology. (Actually, the most common remark was "AMAZING !")